The characters and events portrayed in this book are fictitious. Any similarity to real persons, living or dead, is coincidental and not intended by the author. Any reference to real locations is only for atmospheric effect, and in no way truly represents those locations.

Cover design by Miblart

Published by Higher Bank Books

BATTLE THE DARKNESS

Survive the Darkness Book 8

RYAN CASEY

CHAPTER ONE

Oliver ran as fast as he could down the street and prayed to God his boy was okay.

Foster Road used to be a nice street. Tall trees lined the road. It was quiet. Never any trouble around here. A neighbourhood even *he* was envious of, even though it was the street his mother lived on. He didn't keep his envy secret. The pair of them often bickered about which generation "had it easier." Oliver was adamant that his parents were born in a time when it was easy to get a job, easy to buy a house, just generally *easy* to live.

And *his* generation had been dealt a bad hand. Expensive houses. Job scarcity. And a whole host of other social and economic problems.

Didn't stop Mum shaking her head and dismissing him, though. "Snowflakes, the lot of you," she'd say with that smirk on her face.

Looking down Foster Road now, he started to wonder if Mum had been right all along.

Maybe he should have been more grateful for the world he used to live in.

The street was lined with traditional old semi-detached houses. Many of them had been burned down, the air thick with the smell of smoke. Some of them had the windows boarded up to try and keep looters out, but it didn't look like it was doing that great a job of holding them back.

There were cars in the middle of the road, smashed into one another, abandoned. Blood on the street told a thousand tales of lives that had been changed, all in that instant.

New Year's Eve.

The moment the power went out.

The moment everything changed.

Oliver stood in the middle of the street, panting. His breathing was the only thing he could hear. This street had always been quiet. But right now, there was something eerie about it. Something *dead* about it.

He just hoped his boy was okay.

His feet were sore as hell, blistered to buggery. He felt like he'd run a marathon. He guessed he had, in a way. Cycled some of the way but forced to take the last day or so on foot.

Four days. Four days it'd taken him to get here. Four days it'd taken him to make it from south Manchester, where he was attending a New Year's party with a difference...

A bitter taste filled his mouth.

He thought of Kyla.

Of how he'd told her he was just at work.

Of how disappointed he was that he couldn't spend New Year with her and her friends.

And then he thought of Julia, her body, and the things they did to each other, and...

No.

Now wasn't the time to feel guilty about that.

Now was about his boy.

He'd spent enough time on the road feeling guilty about what he'd been up to on the New Year's Eve he was supposed to be spending with Kyla. He didn't need any more guilt right now.

You'll feel enough guilt when you find your mum and your son's bodies...

Fuck. No. He couldn't think like that. Had to just keep his head down. Had to just search for himself.

He swallowed a lump in his dry throat. He hadn't eaten for days. Drank a little along the way but barely got out of the supermarkets alive. People were looting in full force already. Now money had no meaning and supplies were low, the value of something as simple as a bottle of mineral water had skyrocketed.

Again, he didn't care. Because for all his sins, he loved his family.

He would find Billy.

He would find Mum.

And then he could think about Kyla.

He felt guilty for putting his wife lower in his list of priorities than his son and his mum. But there wasn't anything emotional to it. His mum's was closer than home, and he'd been travelling pretty much on foot for four days now.

He'd seen the state the country was in. He'd seen pretty damned clearly this was serious. He'd seen the army in the streets. He'd seen police losing control.

He'd seen a man being kicked to death for a chocolate bar.

The whole community spirit that arose during that first COVID lockdown? Yeah, all that was gone down the shitter now.

He was at Mum's first because he'd been travelling for ages, and it was closer, and there was nothing more to it than that.

Other than the guilt, maybe...

He thought about Kyla. She would've headed this way herself, 'cause Mum was babysitting Billy.

He thought about her getting here first.

And how uncomfortable that made him feel.

'Cause as much as he liked to pretend to himself that everything was okay where Kyla was concerned... it really, really wasn't.

He walked further down this street he once grew up on. In the distance, he saw a lamppost lying across the road, where a car had flown into it. The wreckage of a taxi veering off the road and into Mr Coogan's living room window. Poor old Mr Coogan always sat by the window, staring out at his birds. Oliver dreaded to think what condition he was in now.

He walked further down the street, trying to go quicker, even though his body screamed at him to slow down, to take a breather. His feet were so damned sore, and his legs didn't have much energy left in them. His chest was tight, and he felt like he might have a frigging heart attack.

Keep it calm, Oliver. Keep it calm. You're here now. You've made it.

He walked up to the driveway of his mum's place and stood right in front of it.

He saw the old tree from next door shadowing the overgrown front garden, which he always promised to mow but never got around to. Saw those dead leaves all across the front of the lawn. They used to drive Mum mad. "Them bloody Asians next door," she used to say, making Oliver cringe. "They could trim that tree and keep the bloody leaves for themselves."

He tensed his fists and looked up at her bedroom window.

The curtains were closed.

In fact, they were closed right through the house.

He wanted to believe she was just keeping a low profile.

But he couldn't shake the nagging feeling something was desperately wrong here.

He walked across the drive. Over to the house. Every step he took felt like he was wading through tar.

Keep on going, Oliver. Everything's gonna be okay. Billy's gonna be fine. Mum's gonna be fine.

He tried the front door, but it was locked. Damn it. Always told Mum to lock up, even in the middle of the day, something which wound her the hell up. She came from a different genera-tion. One where you didn't have to worry about burglars or people trying to rip you off. She hadn't quite caught up with the times. Still fell for every damned bank scam. Even sent her debit card out to a nice bloke from Nigeria once, all because he swore her savings were at risk.

Plus, he was a "nice man from the bank," so what was she supposed to believe?

He reached under the plant pot for the spare key, instinctively looking around to check nobody was looking. The road was so quiet. Nothing but the sound of birds, of wind against the trees.

Across the road, over at that young couple's who moved in recently and occasionally brought Mum cake, he swore he saw the bedroom curtains twitch.

He turned back to the house and stuck the key in the lock.

But the damned thing wouldn't turn.

Key in the other side. Goddammit. The one time he wanted his mum's place to be easily accessible, he couldn't even get inside.

He hopped the gate and walked round the side. Didn't see any sign of her through the kitchen window. Back door was locked, too, and he didn't have a spare key.

He'd have to go round the back, into the garden.

But as he walked around into the garden, he froze.

She always sat in the back room.

What if she was in there now?

What if she was dead?

Or what if she wasn't in there at all?

He swallowed a sickly lump in his throat and stepped around the back of the house.

There was no sign of Mum back there, in her usual spot on the sofa. Which both relieved and worried him.

Where was she?

And where was Billy?

He tried the big glass patio doors, but again, no way in. And as he stood back on the slippery decking he always insisted Mum didn't have put down, he realised there was only going to be one way in.

He was going to have to smash the patio windows.

He felt a vandal even thinking about it. Breaking into his old family home.

But hell, what other choice did he have?

He looked around the garden for something he could use. Or maybe he could try the garage. There'd be something in there. One of Dad's old tools he bought and never used.

He went to walk towards it when he noticed Mum's bird table.

Heavy thing. He knew 'cause he'd bought it for her and dropped it on his toe when he was bringing it round. Wasn't one to enjoy embarrassing himself—who was?—but he'd let out a scream that got the attention of the whole damned garden centre.

Kyla laughed for hours about that. Good times.

If only he knew it was just days before her mood swing.

One of her worst ones ever.

The joys of bipolar disorder.

And her other problems, too.

Giving Billy his "medicine." The medicine he didn't really need.

All just to make her feel better. All just to humour her.

He picked up that bird table, being careful to avoid hovering it over his foot this time.

"Well," he said. "Here goes nothing."

He pulled it back and swung it at the patio window.

The glass shattered everywhere. The noise was louder than he expected. A bunch of pigeons in the tree at the bottom of the garden flew off, wings flapping away.

Shit. He didn't want to draw any attention to himself. Especially not like that.

But the window was smashed.

He was in.

He climbed over the loose, broken glass, being careful not to step on any. Saw Mum's newspapers sitting on a pile on the horrible green leather sofa. Old pack of Mini Cheddars spilled out onto the floor.

"Definitely something off," he said, his heart picking up. "No way would you not finish a bag of cheddars."

He walked through into the hallway, which was always so bright and airy. Played with a little football in this hall so many times with Billy when he was younger. The laughs they'd have here.

A lump in his throat.

"I'll find you, lad. I'll find you."

He reached the bottom of the stairs.

Mum's stairlift was still at the top.

Which meant she hadn't come down.

And as Oliver stood there, he had to brace himself. Because he knew what he was going to find. And he knew it wasn't going to be good.

"Mum?" he called. "Billy? It's me. It's Oliver. It's Dad. Every-thing... everything's gonna be okay now."

No sounds.

He climbed up the creaking stairs. Hoped nobody jumped out at him. At least if Billy and Mum were in here, they'd know it was him by now.

"It's only me," he said again. "It's—it's Oliver. It's Dad. It'll be okay now."

He got to the top of the stairs and stopped.

The little bedroom Billy slept in.

The door partly open.

He went to walk towards it when a sudden sour smell struck him.

It was so strong that it made him heave. And he wasn't sure if it was just the smell alone or the realisation of what it was that made Oliver clench his stomach and heave bile all over Mum's recently cleaned carpet.

He lifted himself back up, shaking. Felt like he was going to faint.

You need to be strong, Oliver. Whatever it is... you need to be strong.

He walked to Mum's bedroom door.

Pushed it open.

Be strong.

And then he held his breath and stepped inside.

Mum's room was as peaceful and calm as ever. Birds singing outside. Sunlight peeking in.

Mum lay on the bed.

Quite clearly dead.

Oliver's shaking grew stronger. Tears poured down his face. "Oh, Mum," he said, walking slowly around the side of the bed. "I'm... I'm sorry. I'm sorry."

He walked around to her, still in shock, still not quite believing that this was actually happening to him.

He wanted to hold her despite the smell.

Wanted to kiss her.

He wanted to curl up beside her and feel her warmth, even though her body would be cold now.

But when he reached the side of the bed, he saw something.

A note.

A little note, right on Mum's tummy.

He reached for it. Picked it up.

And when he read it, his whole world fell apart again.

Handwriting.

Handwriting he recognised.

MUM AND DAD,

I know you said never go anywhere without Grandma but I had to go try and find somewhere safer.

I'm hungry and thirsty and scared.
I love you and I miss you and I hope you're okay and hope I'll be okay.
Billy.

OLIVER HELD that note with his shaking hand. Read it, again and again, tears distorting his vision completely.

He was gone.

Billy had left this place, and he was gone.

I'M hungry and thirsty and scared.
I love you and I miss you and I hope you're okay and hope I'll be okay.

HE LOOKED OVER THE NOTE, over at his mum lying there, dead in her bed.

The ringing in his ears grew louder.

His heart beat so fast he couldn't breathe.

"No," he said. "No..."

He went to turn around.

But all the strength left Oliver's body.

He fell to his mother's side.

Held on to her cold, smelly body.

Put her limp, bony hand on his head.

And Oliver lay there, gripped onto Billy's note, and he cried.

CHAPTER TWO

* * *

Aoife saw the smoke rising in the distance and felt her stomach sink.

It was late afternoon. The sun would be setting soon. The days were getting a bit longer, sure, but still not long enough. She still felt freezing cold all the time. Shivering in the freezing cold was basically her default state at this stage.

But looking ahead, she felt a knot in her stomach. 'Cause she knew the weather was the least of her problems right now.

She saw that smoke rising from the remains of the old town before her. Smoke was always bad news. Because smoke meant other people.

And other people were a risk. They were a threat.

And that might be something she could handle on her own.

But when she was looking after someone like Billy… well, things were different.

"What should we do?"

Aoife looked around and saw Billy crouching there beside her. They were behind a rusty old Renault Clio. Through the window, Aoife could see a bottle of clear liquid with all green, yellow gunk floating to the surface. A baby's bottle, once upon a time. A car seat.

She didn't want to look too closely, but she swore she saw a skeleton inside it.

She looked over the top of the car, over towards that smoke in the distance. The road was cracked. The buildings up ahead looked empty. The grass at the side of the road was overgrown as nature took control again. It'd grow even more now spring was approaching. Right now, it gave her extra shelter. Extra protection from whoever might be in the middle of that town. Watching.

The smell of smoke was strong in the air. Didn't smell good. Damp logs, by the smell of things. Taste of it got right to the back of Aoife's throat. Along with the taste of blood.

"We go around the town," Aoife said. "No other choice. Come on."

She started to walk around the side of the car when she realised she didn't hear any footsteps following her.

She sighed and turned around. "Billy."

Billy stared at the road. "I thought we were trying to find somewhere safe?"

"We are trying to find somewhere safe."

"Then can't we at least take a look?"

"Trust me," Aoife said. "There's nothing to see here."

"But—"

"No buts. Come on. It isn't safe here."

"How do you know?"

"I just do, okay?"

Billy opened his mouth. For a second, it looked like he was going to say something.

Then he just closed his mouth and nodded. Lowered his head and followed Aoife.

She felt bad for a moment. Poor kid just had a dose of that dangerous commodity called hope, and she couldn't hold that against him.

"I'm just thinking about you," Aoife said.

But he didn't even look up at her as he walked past her. Sulked along in front of her.

Whatever. Suit yourself.

She looked over towards that smoke again and wondered. What if it *was* just an ordinary group? What if it *was* someone who could offer her and Billy safety? Security? Didn't matter how permanent that safety and security were. There was little such thing as permanence in the world. Always been the case, but that fact was all the more obvious these days.

She felt that curiosity herself, though. Tugging her over towards that place. Making her want to scout it out, to see for herself.

Then she felt a knot in her stomach.

A knot painful and tight enough to stop her interest dead in its tracks.

She turned away from the smoke and saw Billy walking off ahead. A bit too far out of her reach for comfort.

"Hey," Aoife said.

Billy didn't slow down.

"Little brat," she muttered.

She jogged over to him. Her legs were stiff, and her body was sore. Wasn't long ago she'd been beaten like hell by that psychopath Ramiro, after all. At least he was gone.

And God knows whether that Jarrod bloke who'd stormed in and replaced him would be any better. It didn't matter. One day, someone stronger than him would come along, and the cycle would go on, and on, and on, until the end of fucking time.

She wasn't playing a part in any of that anymore.

"Billy," Aoife said. "Wait up."

But Billy still wasn't slowing down.

He kept on walking.

"Disobedient little…"

Aoife stopped.

Stopped right in her tracks.

Because she saw something.

Or rather, someone.

A silhouette.

A silhouette right beside that green car.

The car Billy was about to step in front of.

She didn't even think.

She lifted her knife.

Ran to the back of the car.

"Billy, stop!"

But it was too late.

The man jumped out.

Grabbed Billy.

Rugby tackled him to the ground.

"Get the fuck off him!" Aoife shouted. Fully aware she'd be drawing attention to herself. But too terrified for Billy's safety to care.

The man grabbed Billy. Lifted him up. He was a real tramp by the looks of things. Greasy, curly hair. Sores all over his skin. Looked like he hadn't had a bath years before the blackout and definitely hadn't had one since.

He held Billy close. "He's mine now."

Aoife gritted her teeth. Looked over at Billy as this man held his dirty hand over his mouth, Billy's eyes staring back at her, wide and terrified.

"Just put him down," Aoife said. "Put him down, and we can talk about this."

But the man stood his ground and shook his head. "He's mine. You can't take him away. Not after—not after what happened to my other boy. You can't... you can't keep taking 'em away from me like this."

And then Aoife realised the man's initial anger and aggression had turned into sadness.

The tears rolling down his red face.

The sound of his teeth chattering as he rocked Billy from side to side.

"I just want my boy," he said. "I just—I just want my boy."

Aoife took a deep breath. Nodded. Then she lowered her knife. "I know," she said. Walking closer and closer to Billy. Keeping her calm. Keeping things as cool as possible. "But this boy... this isn't your boy."

"He can be!" the man shouted.

"Maybe he can," Aoife said. Still walking towards him. "Maybe... maybe you can come with us, and he can be your boy. And you can have a family again. Hmm? How does that sound?"

The man narrowed his eyes. He looked around, almost as if he could see other people approaching him. Lunatic, clearly.

"Come on," Aoife said. "This isn't going to get you anywhere, and you know it. Put the boy down, and we can talk. It doesn't have to be this way."

She got closer to him until, eventually, she was within touching distance.

She looked right into his bloodshot eyes, and she smiled.

"Put him down. That's it. You can do it."

And the man did.

He started to loosen his grip on Billy.

Started to lower him to the ground.

"I just—I just get scared," he said. "I just get scared, and I get sad, and—"

He didn't finish what he was saying.

Because Aoife rammed the blade into his chest.

"Aoife!" Billy shouted.

She held the man close to her. Smelled his stench. Felt disgusted by the sight of him.

The thought of those filthy fingers on Billy's body...

"You did this," she said, peering right into his wide eyes as he started to shake, as blood trickled down his chin. "You did."

And then she yanked the knife from his chest and watched him fall to the ground.

She looked down at him. Watched him splutter and shake. Wiped her knife on his coat.

And then she looked around at Billy, into his startled eyes, and she grabbed his hand.

"Now come on," she said, seeing movement over towards the smoke in the distance. "We're getting out of here."

———————

CHAPTER THREE

———————

Aoife and Billy walked down the train tracks, and neither of them said a word.

The sun was setting right up ahead. Real gorgeous orange glow. Would've looked nice once upon a time. She might've taken a few photos of it, put the best ones on Instagram. Might've even stood by Jason's side and drank a glass of wine as they watched it shimmer on the horizon.

But nowadays, sunset was always bad news.

Because sunset meant night.

And you didn't want to be out at night. Nobody did.

She knew it was weird. A psychological thing, really. Probably went back to old habits. 'Cause of all the people she'd met since the beginning of this great blackout, nobody was keen on travelling at night.

It only seemed to be the most harmful and the ones you wanted to avoid who were out here when it got late.

She walked across the slippery train tracks, her footsteps crunching against the icy ground. Looked like it was going to be another cold night. Winter hadn't loosened its grip just yet then. She hoped the signs of spring weren't just a false dawn. It felt like this winter had dragged on a hell of a lot longer than any she could remember.

Not to sound sentimental or pathetic, but the arrival of spring brought hope. Hope that she could find somewhere for Billy and her to settle down and live. Somewhere they didn't have to worry about who or what they were going to bump into, at least for a while, anyway.

At the same time, an instinctive sense of dread, right at the pit of her gut.

The thought of something happening to Billy.

The thought of losing him.

And the thought of going to some other place with him—some place that would inevitably bill itself as "safe." But was anywhere safe in this world, really?

She'd seen Sanctuary fall to a band of thugs. And that place was supposed to be the future.

Who was to say the district she was heading towards in Rhyl would be any better?

If that's where she was heading at all...

Billy was quiet. He had his head down. He hadn't looked at Aoife since the run-in on the road earlier, let alone spoken to her.

Which wasn't especially strange. He was a pretty quiet kid.

But Aoife wasn't an idiot. She could tell when something was off.

And it didn't take a genius to figure out what it was.

She looked down at the blood crusted on her palms. She could smell it in the air. Not just her own blood anymore, but that man's blood on the road.

The crazy who'd grabbed Billy.

She didn't regret what she did. He was a danger. A threat to the pair of them. He couldn't be trusted.

And he was living in total misery. So really, in the end, she'd done the kindest thing.

She looked ahead of Billy. Saw a train in the middle of the

tracks, abandoned long ago. A few crows circling it. "We should shelter in there for the night. Looks safe enough."

Billy didn't say a word.

Aoife gritted her teeth. She wasn't getting involved in games like this. If the little shit wanted to sulk, he could sulk.

She knew she should stay quiet, but she couldn't resist. "Want some water?"

Again, no response.

Ignorant bastard. She was trying to help him out here.

She knew she should resist, but she couldn't help herself.

"Look, if you're just gonna sulk all night, that's fine. Totally fine. But I'm trying here, Billy. I'm trying for you, and I'm trying for both of us. But, sure. If you want to sulk, that's fine with me. No fucking problem."

"You shouldn't have killed that man," Billy said.

Aoife sighed. She knew it was about him. "That man tried to hurt you. And he would've done if I hadn't done something."

"You don't know that," Billy said.

"I *know* he rugby-tackled you to the ground. I *know* he was insane and unstable. And I *know* that if I hadn't done what I did, he would've hurt you. And if not you, someone else. I did him a favour, I did everyone else a favour, and I did you a favour."

"I don't want your favours," Billy muttered.

"What was that?"

"I said..."

"Actually, I heard you. You don't want my favours. Well, go on. Be my guest. 'Cause I didn't ask you to trail along with me. I was doing perfectly fine on my own before you came along."

She regretted those words right away. Shit.

Billy looked at her with tearful eyes.

"Billy," she said. "I didn't—"

"You *weren't* doing fine," he snapped. "You were imagining your dead friend and your dead dog. If I hadn't come along, you'd still be doing that. But—but you're still miserable. And you're still nasty. And you're still cruel."

Aoife froze. She stood totally still as Billy walked on. She expected him to react with sadness. But the things he'd just said... what he'd just said right now... it stunned her. Fucking floored her.

She was *not* expecting that level of anger.

Billy walked on towards the train.

Aoife stood there, watching the sun's orange glow grow dimmer and dimmer.

And all she could do was think of those words.

You weren't doing fine... you're still miserable. And you're still nasty. And you're still cruel.

And as she stood there, lump in her throat, Aoife knew Billy was right.

CHAPTER FOUR

Once they were inside the abandoned train, Aoife and Billy didn't speak again.

It was a strange environment, an old train like this. One of those reminders of just how things used to be when they were normal—an empty few cans of beer lying on their side, probably from some lads on their way out on New Year's Eve. A pair of pink rabbit ears on one of the seats, from a hen do or a fancy-dress party. A newspaper dated 31st December, sitting there on one of the seats.

All these reminders of how things used to be. How *normal* things used to be.

But then they were contrasted with other things, things more of this new world. Specks of rat shit all over the tables. The smell of damp. Mould creeping up the windows. Freezing cold air.

Aoife sat in one of the table seats and wrapped her arms around her chest for warmth. Billy sat opposite her. His eyes were closed, but she knew he wasn't asleep.

Mostly because he kept opening an eye and peeking at her to see if she was awake.

She could play this damned game all night. What Billy said to her about being crazy and being mean. It'd got to her. Upset her, in all truth.

She knew she should just ignore it. He was a kid, after all. And when kids were tired, and they'd been through shit—when *anyone* was tired and had been through shit—they could say things they didn't mean. Aoife knew that herself. She'd put her foot in it a fair few times in her life already, and just earlier with Billy.

But she thought about what he said. About her being crazy without him. About her being mean. And how she'd told him to do one because she was just fine without him. She shouldn't have said that, and she knew it.

Billy opened an eye again to peek out of, then closed it the second he realised Aoife was looking.

"Neither of us are doing a very convincing job of pretending to sleep, huh?"

Billy didn't say a word in response.

Aoife sighed. "Look, Billy. I'm sorry for what I said. I shouldn't have said that. I was just... I was trying to protect you from that man. I know you said we should've given it a chance. But I see things differently. Quite frankly, look at where you ended up and look at where I ended up. You ended up with Ramiro, and I didn't. So forgive me if I trust my own judgement over yours."

Billy kept his eyes closed. But he was breathing harder now.

Aoife shook her head and stretched. "Look. I don't like trying to sleep on an argument. Always liked to resolve things and always have. Don't like it when there's something on my mind. So I... I'm sorry for how I acted. Sorry for killing that guy. Sorry for saying what I said to you."

"But do you mean it?" Billy said, out of nowhere.

"What?"

"Are you really sorry? Or are you just saying that?"

Aoife shrugged. "What does it matter, really? Sure. Yeah, I mean it. That better?"

Billy closed his eyes again, shook his head.

"What do you want, kid? I've said I'm sorry. I'm here looking after you, and I'm taking you someplace safe. And if we don't get someplace safe, then we'll make it on our own. I didn't mean what I said. About being... about being fine before you came along. I know that's not the case. But this world isn't a good world. You know that just as well as I do. *More* than I do. So when I say someone's bad, you trust me. I might do something you aren't keen on. I might do something you don't like. But I'll do it because I'm looking out for you. I'm looking out for both of us."

"Are you sure?" Billy asked.

His eyes were open again now. He was staring right at Aoife. Staring deeply into her eyes. Made her feel self-conscious and weird. So much so she had to look away.

"Sure about what?"

But this time, Billy didn't say anything.

This time, he shook his head, closed his eyes, and lay across the seats.

"We should sleep," he said. "Sorry too."

She wanted to ask Billy more about what he was asking. She wanted to talk things out more.

But at the same time... he'd given her that apology, and she'd apologised to him, and she had to leave things at that.

For now, at least.

"Goodnight, kid," she said.

Billy didn't say anything back.

She sat there and looked out of the cracked, dusty train window, out into the darkness.

She knew she wasn't getting much sleep tonight.

CHAPTER FIVE

Carlton tightened his grip around the man's throat until he was absolutely sure there was no life left in the bastard.

It was always such an empowering feeling, depriving another man of his life. Went right back to when he was a kid, actually. Used to sit outside with a magnifying glass and shine it around the ants on a hot summer's day. At first, they'd just be wandering around, going about their business. And then, as he weaved that beam of light between them, they started to panic. Started to feel the cracked concrete getting hotter around them. Every now and then, he'd move that light to within a millimetre of one of those ants, and they'd scuttle off in the opposite direction.

And his heart started racing, his legs started to shake.

And even though he didn't know what was happening at the time, his dick started getting hard.

As he held on to this man and squeezed so so tight, he got that same feeling. All of those same feelings.

He saw his bloodshot eyes staring up at him. The poor bloke had strained for breath so much that he'd burst a load of blood vessels. Thick saliva laced with blood drooled down his chin. His teeth chattered away as he opened his mouth, tried to say some-thing, tried to beg and plead.

His hands kept on slapping against the back of Carlton's. Hard at first. Nasty at first.

But now weak. Desperate.

Like he was begging.

Pleading.

And that made Carlton smile even more.

Made him even harder.

That thought he might be able to give this bloke a little hope before it all ended for him... that was the most beautiful thought of all.

It reminded him of the first time he'd killed an animal. A cat, it was. Found it sitting at the side of a road. Load of kittens by its side. At first, he was amazed. Seemed weird, seeing it there in the middle of nowhere, a load of kittens with it. You never really think of nature as doing its thing until you see it for yourself. I mean, have you ever seen cats fucking? No. And if you have, you're a fucking pervert.

So suddenly seeing this bundle of eight cats circling their mother... yeah, that was something.

But it wasn't right. It looked lost. He used to have a long walk down a country lane to get back home from school. Barely any houses down there, so they were a long way from home.

He looked at the cats sitting there on the grass, and he remembered hearing something about Mrs Dawlish's cat going missing. One of the teachers from school. And come to think of it, this cat did look a lot like hers. Mrs Dawlish was one of the nicer teachers. Didn't treat him like a weirdo. So she'd be so happy with him if he brought her cats back. Might even go easier on him during his next science test.

But then he felt that other urge inside.

That urge he'd always had.

The urge that had been there right since the day he'd pushed his brother off the top of a slide on the playground, leaving him needing stitches in his head.

That urge for power.

That urge to be cruel.

He walked over to those cats.

Looked down at them all.

Smiled.

Mrs Dawlish never did find her cats.

She never even knew her kitty had a litter.

Some mysteries are never solved.

But the power Carlton felt for being the only one to know exactly what'd happened... that was something.

He zoned back into the moment.

Realised he'd loosened his grip on the man's throat, just a little.

Heard him wheezing. Gasping. Coughing up blood.

"Pl... please," he said. "Don't... don't do this. You don't... you don't have to do this. I'll give you anything. Please."

And it was those words that really amused Carlton.

The thought that this man had anything to give.

And the thought that he could give him exactly what Carlton wanted.

Carlton leaned in towards him.

Looked right into his eyes.

"That's a nice sentiment," he said. "But there's only one thing you can give me. And that's exactly what I'm going to take from you."

The man's eyes widened. "No. Pl—"

Carlton squeezed.

Tight.

And then tighter, and tighter, and tighter.

He felt the man shaking.

Felt him slamming his hands against his arms.

Digging his fingernails in.

He just closed his eyes, held on, took a deep breath of the cold winter air, a faint smell of burning in the distance, and he smiled.

It took the man a minute to stop writhing and shaking.

When he stopped, Carlton opened his eyes.

Looked down at him lying there. Lifeless.

And for a moment, he felt release.

For a moment, he felt calm again.

They talk about post nut clarity. Well this was post fucking *murder* clarity.

He closed the man's eyes and folded his arms across his chest.

He rested in that state of euphoria for God knows how long. Until it went dark, anyway.

And then when he started to realise he needed somewhere to shelter, he got up and walked.

In the distance, the train tracks loomed.

CHAPTER SIX

Aoife was standing outside a large, steel wall, which towered over her.

She had no idea how she'd got here. But this wall was big. Huge. So tall it went right up into the sky. Made her dizzy to look up at, so she tried not to do that.

Billy stood by her side. He looked happy. He was saying something, his mouth moving, but Aoife couldn't hear him.

When she looked around, she saw a line of people standing on the grass in front of that steel wall. The sun shone down brightly from above. It was warm, and the sky was bluer than she'd ever seen. It looked like this wall was hiding some kind of community. Like one of the districts, only the walls were far bigger, far better guarded.

"You'll be safe here," a man said. Smiling. Everyone else smiling. All of them dressed in white. Like some kind of cult. "Everyone is safe here."

And Aoife knew she should feel happy. Because she'd made it. She'd found somewhere safe. And it looked like it really, truly was safe.

But something was stopping Aoife walking towards these people.

Something stopping her from letting Billy walk towards these people.

Fear.

"Come on," a woman said. Blonde hair. Blue eyes. Looked perfect. So clean. Glowing. Glowing like only someone from the world before glowed.

And then Aoife saw the people behind this woman, behind this man. Like a big glass window opened up in the wall and she saw everything behind.

She saw Kayleigh.

She saw Rex.

She saw Max.

They were all smiling. And they all looked pristine. They all looked perfect. They all looked happy.

"Come on," Max said. Or maybe it was Kayleigh. Or hell, maybe it was even Rex, she wasn't sure. "It's okay here. It's safe here. Come on..."

And then their faces shifted.

Just for a moment, their faces shifted.

The perfect blonde woman's smile dropped, and Aoife saw a decaying, skeletal figure hiding behind the mask.

Max changed to Ramiro.

Kayleigh changed to Grace.

All of them shifted, just for a moment.

The sky went from bright blue to dark grey.

She tightened her grip on Billy's hand because even though things were bright and sunny again, this wasn't right. They couldn't go in there. Because it wasn't safe. It wasn't what it looked like on the surface.

But she realised when she tightened her grip on Billy's hand that he wasn't there anymore.

His hand just disappeared under her grip.

And when she looked around for him, she saw he was already gone.

"Billy," she said. "What…"

She looked ahead and saw he was already halfway towards those people.

Towards that wall.

"Billy!"

She tried to walk towards them, but her feet were stuck. She looked down and realised she was a part of a wall herself, now. All steel. All steel, and she couldn't move.

She looked up and saw faces. Faces in that steel wall opposite, just like hers.

All of them smiling.

All of them happy.

And Billy walking along, right in front.

"It's okay," a dark, silhouetted figure said. "He's okay now. He'll be safe now."

He reached for Billy's hand.

"Billy!" Aoife screamed.

Billy reached up for the man's hand.

"Billy!"

His fingers touched the man's silhouetted hand.

"Billy!"

"Aoife?"

Aoife opened her eyes. Her heart raced. Billy. The man had him. The man had him, and she was stuck in the wall and—

"Aoife," Billy said. "It's—it's okay. You were just dreaming. Just a nightmare."

Aoife saw Billy in front of her. It was dark, but it was definitely him. She looked around. Looked at the seats, at the aisle. A train. Shit. She was still in the train. It was just a dream. She was okay.

She leaned forward, panting, trying to catch her breath. The dream had fucked with her. Thoroughly fucked with her. She definitely wouldn't be going back to sleep tonight. Didn't want to.

"What were you dreaming about?" Billy asked.

"It doesn't matter. Just a nightmare. Get... get some sleep."

"You were going crazy. I was asleep. You woke me."

Aoife felt her face heating up a bit, flushing. "Don't worry about it. Like I said. Just a dream. Go on. Get some sleep. We've got some more walking to do tomorrow."

Billy was quiet. Aoife's heart raced. She was still shaken up about everything. That dream was screwed up. And as much as she didn't believe in dream meanings and all that shit... she couldn't help seeing some truth in what she'd seen.

The fear.

The fear she had about finding someplace.

And the fear she had about trusting anyone.

It was like all her old fears had come back to bite her all over again—only stronger than ever now.

"I get bad dreams too," Billy said.

Aoife's stomach turned. "I thought you'd gone back to sleep."

"Sometimes... sometimes they're exactly what happened. Sometimes he's beating me. Ramiro. Or one of the others. Or sometimes... sometimes it's worse. Doing the real bad things."

Aoife felt sick. She didn't want to hear this.

But she couldn't tell Billy to be quiet because it made her feel uncomfortable.

She had to be here for him.

"And sometimes in the dreams it's worse. It's even scarier. But now... but now I know it's a dream when I'm dreaming. Now I know. And I always wake up at the end of it."

Aoife listened. But it didn't sound like Billy was going to say anything else.

"You can always talk to me," Aoife said. "About anything. You know that. Right?"

Billy sighed. "I know," he said. "And you can too."

He waited. Aoife waited.

Silence.

Total silence.

Silence Aoife wanted to fill by talking to Billy.

But she was here to be strong for him.

"Goodnight, Billy," she said.

A pause. And then, "Goodnight."

She watched him lean back over onto that chair.

And this time, as she sat there, heart still racing, she felt a little more comfortable about falling to sleep.

Now I know it's a dream when I'm dreaming. Now I know. And I always wake up at the end of it.

CHAPTER SEVEN

This time, when Aoife woke, she didn't feel anywhere near the same degree of anxiety because Billy was right in front of her.

It was bright. Her head ached like mad. Never liked sleeping upright. She knew she could hardly complain. There weren't exactly many luxuries in this world anymore. But she felt like shit. Dry mouth, funny taste of vomit at the back of her throat. Hint of blood, too, from where she'd had her teeth bashed out—something that'd happened not all that long ago at the hands of Ramiro and his gang of thugs.

It seemed like forever ago. Like the previous season in a television series, or some shit like that. She smirked to herself. At least she found her own jokes funny. Always helped.

Billy sat there with a smile on his face. He looked healthier today, somehow. Didn't have those same big bags under his eyes. Clearly had a thoroughly decent sleep, exactly what he needed.

"What're you smirking at?" Aoife asked.

He looked away, clearly trying to avoid eye contact. "I'm not smirking at anything."

"You are. I know a smirk when I see one. Don't think I don't."

He looked back at her. Held eye contact, just for a second. Then looked away again.

She shook her head. Laughed a little. It was good to see him smiling, especially after their argument yesterday. That shit was good for nobody.

The sooner they forgot about that, the better.

The sooner they could just move on from all of that, the better.

"I got you something," Billy said.

Aoife frowned. "Got me something? Where did you order it, Amazon Prime?"

He lifted his hand and opened it up.

In the middle of it, Aoife saw something that made her smile widen even more.

It was a Freddo bar. One of the old Cadburys chocolate treats, a mainstay of any childhood. The packet looked a little frayed at the edges, and the chocolate in the middle looked like it'd been melted and frozen a million times.

But seeing it, this relic of the old world—this relic of youth—which she hadn't seen for so many years now... it made her whole body feel weirdly soft.

"Where did you find that?"

"Just at the front of the train," Billy said.

"I told you not to go..."

She stopped. Because he was here, and he was unscathed.

And he'd brought her a fucking Freddo bar back. What more could she possibly want?

"Thank you," Aoife said. "That's... sweet."

"Is that a pun?" Billy asked.

"What?"

"You said 'that's sweet.' About a Freddo. Is that a pun?"

Aoife felt herself blushing a little. She definitely hadn't intended that. "No," she said. "I don't make puns."

"Why?" Billy asked. "Are they too toffee for you?"

"What even is that?"

"Toffee. Tough. They sound the same, right?"

"They definitely do not sound the same."

"They sound close to the same."

"They do not sound close to the same."

She took the Freddo from him. Moved it around in her hand. "You sure you don't want this?"

"It's okay," Billy said, wiping his mouth.

"Oh. I see how it is. Made sure you fed yourself first, did you?"

"That's what you'd have told me to do. To survive."

Aoife smiled. Nodded. "Fair point."

She unwrapped the chocolate bar. It looked even worse now than before. It'd gone grey. Definitely off.

But fuck. Imagination could do some of the legwork here.

"Well," Aoife said. "Here goes nothing but the shits to look forward to later."

"Gross," Billy said.

She closed her eyes and took a bite out of the Freddo.

It wasn't fresh. To be honest, it didn't really taste of much. And the texture was all lumpy.

But if she really focused enough, she could imagine it was just as rich and tasty as it would've been when her brother, Seth, stole her one from the newsagents when they were just kids.

Stole them, then made her take the blame for it. Bastard.

"How is it?" Billy asked.

Aoife tilted her head. "It's not toad-tally revolting."

Billy frowned. "What?"

"Toad-tally. Totally. You know. Because..."

"But he's a frog. Not a toad."

"You know what? Forget it."

"Don't you mean Frog-get it?"

"No," Aoife said. "No, I absolutely do not."

She shook her head, tried to hide her smile. Finished off her

Freddo. Looked outside, beyond the dirty, smeared windows, past the train tracks, and at the trees beyond.

"What now then?" Billy asked.

Aoife felt a lump swell in her throat. A reminder that they actually had to go somewhere. That they had to find somewhere safe. She'd promised Billy that much. And she wasn't going to let him down.

But then...

That rival part of her. That part of her which enjoyed those small moments like right here, right now. The Freddos for breakfast. The crappy puns.

She didn't want that to end.

And yet she knew she couldn't just drift through the wilderness with this boy. She owed it to him to try and find somewhere. A community. Somewhere safe.

And she owed it to herself to try and trust somebody else. Even if she found it impossible.

"We see what else we can find lying around on here. If there's a Freddo on board, there's a good chance there'll be a whole lot else. You don't just leave Freddos lying around at the end of the world."

"And then?" Billy asked.

Aoife looked at him. Swallowed that lump in her throat. "We go from there when we get there," she said.

Billy opened his mouth. Then he closed it. Smiled. Nodded.

"Come on," he said. "I'll show you where I found the Freddos."

He ran off down the creaky carriage, through the dust, past the smeared windows.

And Aoife stood there and watched him. Smiled.

"Aoife?" he said. "Come on."

She nodded. And then she wiped a tear from her eye. "Coming," she said.

She walked down the carriage, following in Billy's footsteps.

She wanted this moment to last forever.

She wanted it to be just the pair of them for as long as she stayed alive.

Her prayers weren't going to be answered.

They were going to be challenged even sooner than she thought.

CHAPTER EIGHT

Carlton woke up, and his first thought was of murder.

He was... unsatisfied. That was the only way to describe it. There was an emptiness inside. A desire. An urge. Call it whatever you want to call it; the end result is the same. Usually, after a kill, he was satiated for a few days at the very least. Like a hungry lion capturing its prey, savouring the fruits of its labour.

It used to be a lot longer, of course. Like anything, that initial buzz takes a while to wear off. And it used to take a lot less to satisfy him, too. Insects. Rodents. Pets. Old dementia patients in the care homes he used to work in, barely even living. The disabled.

Then... yeah. The fit and the healthy.

But as he lay there under a mouldy old blanket in the little train station at the side of the tracks, he felt that familiar feeling.

A sense of needing something more.

He gulped. What came next? That's what worried him. What happened when he didn't get the kick he used to get from murdering the average Joe on the street? Where did he go from there?

He figured he'd just kill himself in the end when it all got too much. After all, what was there that was greater or more rewarding to kill than the average, well-to-do person? And he'd killed tons of them now. Women, first. Then men, because he hated them more and he wanted to build up to them.

But where did he go from here?

He got up. Stepped out into the fresh air from the cold, damp station shelter. Looked down the railway tracks. Maybe he was just hungry. Maybe he just hadn't slept well.

But no. That sense of unease, right at the pit of his stomach. No point kidding himself. He knew exactly what it was.

He needed... more.

Multiple people at once? He wasn't sure. Even that sounded a bit light. Like a ready meal or some fast food, and not the full three-course Michelin starred meal he needed right now.

He hopped down onto the train tracks. Listened to the crows cawing. It was a nice day. Bright. Sunny. Felt more like spring than winter. He tried to focus on the good things. Tried to enjoy the sun, the warmth. Tried to enjoy the fact that soon, things would be getting better. Spring and summer were always easier. They always had been. It was the same when he was a kid. His dad was always around less in spring and summer because of his work. Carlton didn't know what he did. He never told him. Neither did Mum. Probably just off on some affair or other on Mum's earnings, in all truth.

But he'd always seem to be home at winter.

And when he was home and trapped in the house with Carlton and Mum... he was mean.

He took a deep breath, pushed that anxiety away.

He's gone now, Carlton.

He's gone.

And he's never coming back.

You're twice the man he ever was.

He walked down the tracks and tried to focus on the positives

—on the sun, and the fact that he was alive, and that he wasn't *too* hungry or thirsty, all things considered. His therapist always told him keeping a gratitude list was important.

But his therapist was also a hypocritical moron who had a nervous breakdown and went around noshing off half the city when her husband left. So who the fuck was she to give him advice?

No, there was no getting past his hunger. There was no getting past his desire. It was actually making him shake.

He was sweating, even though he was freezing cold.

He needed someone.

He needed something he couldn't even describe.

He needed something he couldn't even put his finger on.

But he didn't feel like he would have much luck finding it.

He tensed his fists and bit his lip so hard he tasted blood. And that just made it worse.

Because for a moment, just for a moment, he got a glimpse of the violence he needed satisfying.

He got a literal taste of blood.

He staggered down the train tracks when he saw something that stopped him... well, in his tracks.

There were two people up ahead.

A woman.

And by her side, a boy.

He looked young. Ten? Fifteen? Hard to tell. Skinny. Nubile.

And just seeing him unlocked a world of possibilities for Carlton.

Just seeing him made him realise he'd been wrong to think he'd run out of options.

That he'd run out of possibilities.

Children.

They were an area he'd never touched.

They were a taboo he'd never indulged in.

They were a killing he'd never committed.

He looked at that boy, and he moved his tongue over his lips as that desire grew stronger, as his heart pumped faster.

He smiled.

He knew exactly what he wanted now.

And in this world, Carlton always got what he wanted.

Always.

CHAPTER NINE

"So. Can we talk about where we're going yet?"

Aoife sighed the second Billy said those words. They'd managed to walk for a whole hour down the train tracks without him bringing up the elephant in the room of where they were heading towards. Of course, she knew the topic was always going to come up eventually. And she knew realistically she only had one feasible answer. Rhyl. The district in North Wales where they'd constructed something like Sanctuary.

Only she had no idea what sort of state it was in. She had no clue whether it was even still standing. She had no idea if the Order of Light had managed to keep the power online, whether they'd been able to expand, or if they'd just ended up toppled after all.

She had no idea. She sure hadn't seen any evidence of advancement on the scale she'd seen at Sanctuary anywhere around the country in the eighteen months since she'd left that place.

Could be nothing. Britain was a big place when you were travelling on foot, after all.

But even so... did she really have any other choice?

Scotland? There was another district up there. Another chance for hope.

But that seemed way too far away right now.

She focused on the train tracks, walking from one to the other like she used to do as a kid. Pretended the floor was lava beneath. The sun in the blue sky above was actually quite bright, and the bulk of the snow had melted. Felt like spring. Not warm but getting there.

"Aoife?"

"Sorry," Aoife said, looking around at Billy, who walked alongside her. She kept on forgetting she had company. Weird, in a way. She'd spent so long alone that having company was somewhat novel.

Even though she'd spent so much time convincing herself that she *had* the company of Kayleigh and Rex.

Kayleigh and Rex who were gone. Long, long gone.

"It's like I said," Aoife said. "There's... there's a place in Wales. A place called Rhyl. There's a community there. Apparently. A community who have power. Electricity. Not too different to the old world."

Billy's eyes widened, like he couldn't believe what Aoife was saying. "Do they have, like, Xboxes and stuff?"

Aoife laughed. "I can't guarantee Xboxes. But... but it's as close to how things used to be as I've come across."

"How do you know about it?"

Aoife gulped. A bitter taste to her mouth. A chill wind brushing against her. "It's like I said. I came from one of those places."

"Why would you leave?"

Aoife stopped walking right away. Almost immediately, thick clouds appeared overhead, out of nowhere. The wind was picking up, getting cooler. Seemed like snow was on the way. "Where'd this come from?"

"Why would you leave?"

Aoife looked at Billy, and she knew she had to tell him the full truth. She'd told him bits. And she'd pretty much run through things before in heated moments. But the actual full truth? That's something she hadn't completely got off her chest.

So she told him everything as they walked into the rapidly worsening conditions. She told him about being forced to kill her psychopathic brother, Seth. About what happened to Max. And then about Grace. She told him about Kayleigh, the fight against Robert's cult, and Sanctuary. She told him about what happened there—about Gregg's death, Harvey falling, Yuri's betrayal, and his power grab.

And then she told him about the moment she pointed the gun to the power source and destroyed everything Harvey and the Order of Light had been working towards.

Losing Kayleigh and Rex.

And then the eighteen months alone since.

He listened. Didn't say a word. And she felt judged. She felt totally exposed. Being so honest and open about everything she'd been through... it felt strange, speaking them out loud.

Because she started to realise she should have no shame for being a little bit fucked up. She'd been through a hell of a lot. More than anyone should have to handle.

But then, who hadn't? Who still alive hadn't been through shit —and got their hands dirty in the process?

But Billy didn't say anything. He didn't look like he was judging.

He just kept on walking, slowly, alongside Aoife.

"No wonder you're scared."

Aoife frowned. "What?"

"Of other people. When you've seen so many bad people. And lost so many good people. I'm just... I'm just saying. No wonder you're scared."

Aoife smiled. She couldn't help herself smiling. "For all you've been through," she said. "Everything you've been through. And you still haven't given up on people. Have you?"

Billy stared into space. Shrugged. "Grandma always said things worked out for the best in the end. Always. Didn't feel like that. When I was with Ramiro. And those men. But... but if I wasn't, I wouldn't be with you. Going to Wales."

He smiled at her. And her throat tightened. A lump in her throat. Tears built again in her eyes. He was so wholesome. So fucking pure.

It actually hurt her just how hopeful and *good* he was.

"That's certainly one way of looking at things," she said.

She looked ahead at the rain lashing down from above.

She hoped it'd stop sometime soon.

"Come on," she said. "If we're going to get to Wales, we'd better get moving."

She held out a hand to him.

He hesitated. Just for a moment, he hesitated.

And then, he took it.

The pair of them walked into the storm.

Overhead, lightning flashed, and thunder erupted...

CHAPTER TEN

The weather didn't get any better, and the thought of getting to Wales any time soon—or any fucking time at all—seemed less and less likely by the hour.

It was fucking unbelievable how fast the skies had changed from blue and spring-like, bringing with it all its hope, to thick, black clouds. Hailstone pelted down from above. Thunder exploded all around. Flashes of lightning lit up the skies, so bright it was blinding. Just up ahead, Aoife saw one of the bolts slam into an old telegraph pole, setting it alight on contact.

Billy looked like he was struggling. He had his arms wrapped around his body like he was trying to hug himself, keep himself warm. But Aoife could hear him shivering from here, poor thing. She wished she could give him a coat or something thicker, but she didn't have one.

And she wasn't feeling too clever herself.

Her face ached. Her mouth ached. Fuck, every inch of her ached. She thought back to Max, right after they'd escaped to his cabin, all those years ago. How that stab wound had burdened him with an infection he was lucky to survive. She'd done so well to go so far without getting herself an injury like that which floored her.

But this felt like it might be the one.

"We're going to have to stop," Aoife said.

Billy looked around. Squinted at her through the hailstone. "What?"

"We're going to have to stop," she shouted, barely able to breathe through the wind. "The weather. It's... it's not getting any better."

"I'm okay," Billy shouted. "I'm—I'm cold, but I'm okay. We'll be fine."

Aoife didn't want to speak the truth to Billy. *But I'm not okay.* Because she didn't want to worry him. He had enough on his plate as it was. The prospect of something happening to her and ending up on his own out here, with only Rhyl in mind?

That was terrifying.

But she didn't want him to know just how much pain she was in, and how much she was hurting... or how weak she was.

"I know you're okay," Aoife said, limping along against the intense winds. The hail smacking against her face, stinging her cheeks. "But this storm. It's... it's not something we want to mess around with."

"It'll be okay," Billy said. "We've got to keep going."

"Billy, it won't be okay. It... I..."

"It'll be okay—"

A bang.

A huge bang, right up ahead.

A flash.

And then Aoife felt herself tumble back, slam against the ground.

Her ears rang. Her head spun. She tasted blood, stronger now than before.

She blinked a few times, tried to understand, tried to squint above and see. Just a big dark circle dominating her vision.

When she blinked a few times, she saw Billy crouched over her.

"Are you okay?"

Aoife shook her head, tried to pull herself to her feet. But her stomach and her legs hurt more than before. Even fucking worse.

"You got hit," Billy said. "The lightning. I don't know if it hit you, but it was close, and—and it's set a fire, look."

Aoife looked at the tracks ahead. Saw they were burning. Smelled smoke in the air. Shuddered. Smell of smoke always triggered her without fail. Too many memories attached to it.

"We've—we've got to get off the tracks," Billy said.

"Yeah. Kind of what I've been trying to tell you, Billy."

"I'm sorry. I didn't—I didn't mean for you to get hurt. I just—"

"It's okay," Aoife said. "It's okay. Let's just get out of here, okay?"

Billy nodded. Walked over to the side of the tracks and hopped up onto the platform. Aoife limped over. Tried to move fast, but her legs ached. Her head spun. She didn't feel good. Not at all.

"Do you need help?" Billy asked.

Aoife stood by the side of the platform, and she felt exhausted. She looked at the raised platform and wanted to grab it, lift herself onto it. But the mere thought of it exhausted her and made her want to collapse.

"I'll be okay," she said.

"You don't look okay."

"I'll be okay, Billy. Alright? I have to be okay."

He lowered his head. Shit. She needed to stop snapping at him. He was the goddamned reason she needed to be okay, after all.

"Sorry," Aoife said. "Just... just give me a sec, and I'll be up there with you. Right?"

Billy looked up at her. Made eye contact for just a second, then looked away.

"I'll be fine," she said. "Don't worry."

She grabbed the sides of the platform. Dragged herself onto it. A harder task than she expected it to be.

But she did it.

Pulled herself onto it and stood up.

She held her ground as the wind battered her, as the hail lashed against her face. As Billy stood there staring at her like he knew something was wrong.

There was something wrong. Very wrong.

That splitting headache.

The blood taste getting stronger and stronger in her mouth.

That dizziness. That exhaustion.

And the wind and the hail getting worse and worse and worse...

"Come on," she said, walking into the wind, almost tumbling forward. Every sound seemed louder than it should be. "We... we have to get to shelter. We can't... we can't keep..."

"Aoife? Are you..."

She didn't hear anything else.

The spinning sensation took over her.

The purple cloud completely covered her vision.

The taste of blood replaced everything else.

And then everything faded away into blackness.

CHAPTER ELEVEN

Billy felt scared again when he watched Aoife pass out and fall over.

It was so windy and rainy. He was so cold. He was tired. So tired. He'd barely slept on the train. Kept on thinking he was seeing things outside the window, in the dark.

Ramiro.

Ramiro coming for him.

Because Ramiro never gave up.

But he'd kept on walking along the train tracks with Aoife because he wanted her to know he was strong. And he'd wanted to keep going because he wanted to find somewhere safe. Somewhere like Aoife spoke of. The place with the electricity. With the power.

He didn't know if he trusted them. Not yet. It was hard to trust anybody when he'd been through the things he'd gone through.

But he trusted Aoife. And right now, that was all that mattered.

But now she was lying on the train platform in front of him, and she didn't look well.

Her nose was bleeding. The blood was diluted from the rain. Her eyes were closed. She looked like she was twitching, like when Charlotte had a seizure back in school, and the whole class stood in the playground and watched as Mrs Dennett tried to hold her still.

And Billy didn't know what to do. He felt scared. Just as scared as he'd felt that day when Ramiro's people first captured him.

Just as scared as he'd felt that day when the power went out.

He felt alone.

But he couldn't just stand here and do nothing.

He had to do something.

"Aoife," he said.

He went over to her side. Tried to shake her, just a little, as the hailstone hammered down and the thunder exploded above him. He wasn't scared of it before when he'd been walking down the tracks. Well. He *was*. But he knew he wasn't alone. He knew he was with someone he could trust. So he'd felt better. Stronger.

Not the cowardly kid people used to always pick on him for being.

He nudged her again, trying desperately to wake her but at the same time not being too hard with her. You weren't supposed to disturb people when they were having a seizure. It could be dangerous, apparently. He didn't know where he'd heard that, but he *had* heard it, so he figured it was good advice.

But as he crouched here, jeans sodden, he felt helpless. Just watching Aoife lying here like this, twitching away. She'd been hurt badly. The lightning struck right near her. Or maybe it hit her. He wasn't sure. All he knew was there was a huge flash and a bang, and then Aoife went flying.

And now she was unconscious.

He wanted to do something to help her. He looked around, squinted. They were lucky that they were on a platform when it happened, or they'd be stuck in the middle of nowhere. There was a shelter just up ahead. Maybe he could drag her in there. Get her out of the rain. He couldn't just leave her here. He had to try something.

"It'll be okay," he said. "I'll—I'll get us out of this."

He went to pull Aoife and tumbled back, smacking his head against the concrete. Tears welled up as the pain grew stronger. Dammit. She wasn't big, but she was heavier than she looked, and he was weaker than he remembered.

"We can do this," he said. "I can do this."

He clenched his jaw and grabbed Aoife under her armpits. And then he pulled her. Pulled her as hard as he could.

His legs shook. His sodden feet could barely hold on to the ground.

But she was moving.

He was moving her just a little bit.

"Come on," he said, as another blast of thunder echoed above. "I've got this. I can do this."

He walked back further, finding it easier now. Not *easy*, but he was getting into the groove of it.

He could get her to the shelter.

He could look after her while she was sick.

"We're going to be okay," he said. "Everything's going to be okay."

He pulled her further along when suddenly he tumbled back again and slipped into a cold, slushy puddle of melted ice.

He bit his tongue. Tasted blood. Let out a little whimper instinctively and felt silly for it right away. That wasn't a strong thing to do. Wasn't a tough thing to do. He needed to be better than that.

He pushed himself back to his feet, and then he stumbled over again. Slipped on the ice.

And he felt useless.

Totally useless.

He was useless out here.

He was no good to Aoife.

He was no good to anybody.

There was one place you weren't useless...

He thought of Ramiro and his people, and he felt a shot of fear in his chest, and he shook his head and squeezed his eyes shut.

"No," he said. "No."

He took a deep breath of the freezing cold air.

"I'm going to do this. I'm going to be strong."

And then he opened his eyes, and he went to drag Aoife towards the shelter again.

When he reached for her to drag her along the remainder of the platform, he saw something in the distance.

Right on the middle of the tracks, there was a man.

Standing there.

Staring at him.

Smiling at him.

CHAPTER TWELVE

Carlton smiled at the boy and felt absolutely certain about what he had to do.

He'd watched the pair of them for a while now. Followed them, not too closely, but not too far away. Didn't want to risk losing them. Or risk losing the boy in particular.

But he also didn't want the hunt to be over too soon. That was part of the entire thrill, after all. Identifying your prey. Stalking it.

And then the final, beautiful moment...

It was like sex without foreplay, otherwise. You didn't just get on with the killing and then be done with it. It had to have a build-up.

Carlton didn't know a lot about sex. Not consensual, anyway. Or with anyone, well. Alive.

But he knew a fuck load about killing.

He'd watched them walk down those tracks as the sun turned to torrential rain, to hailstone, to thunder and lightning and wind. It'd come from nowhere. Made Carlton feel like shit. He really thought spring was on its way earlier.

But fuck. What the hell was he moaning about?

He had absolutely no reason to feel agitated right now.

He had everything he was searching for right in front of him.

The lightning bolt was wild. Watched it break through the sky, whack some telegraph pole up ahead, starting a fire.

And then the next one?

It hit the woman. Well, hit the ground right by her, anyway. Sent her flying back.

He'd watched her get to her feet. Watched her stagger to the platform.

Watched her collapse and watched the boy try to draw her to shelter.

And now, here they were.

The boy and him.

Looking at each other.

Prey looking at predator, realising he was being watched.

And predator looking at prey.

Carlton wanted the whole hunt to last longer. He hadn't had anywhere near enough foreplay. Not yet. He wanted the kid to be afraid. He wanted him to feel fear.

He wanted him to know he was being hunted and to realise that time was running out. That his options were disappearing. He wanted the kid to feel afraid, boxed in, and feel there was no way out.

He wanted this whole thing to last.

And he was going to make it last.

In his own way, he was going to make it last.

He walked down the tracks.

The kid's eyes widened. He didn't say a word. Didn't say anything to Carlton.

Just stood there and stared at him. Watched.

Carlton walked.

Kept on walking.

Not quickly. In no damned rush at all.

Just slowly.

Across the tracks.

One step after another.

And it was only when he'd walked about ten steps that the kid started to struggle.

He lifted the woman. Dragged her as much as he could. Which was quite sweet, Carlton had to admit. Usually, when in fear, a kid would just run. Leave the person they were with.

But something about how this kid was acting reminded him of himself.

Walking in on Mum being beaten by Dad. A fire lit in the kitchen.

Grabbing the iron.

Whacking him across the head.

Burying it into his skull, again and again, and again.

And then dragging Mum out of that house, as it burned.

"I've got you, Mummy. I've got you..."

He looked into the kid's eyes, and he saw a flash of himself in them.

And then he pushed those thoughts away.

He was prey.

He wasn't innocent. Because he was going to grow up to be a man.

And even if he was innocent... what did it matter?

The more innocent, the better.

They made for better killings.

Because they were more fearful. More afraid.

He kept on walking. Slowly. Watching as that boy dragged the woman further and further to that shelter. The shelter was only small. So it didn't matter if he got there. It wasn't like he was going to get away.

Carlton wasn't going anywhere any time soon, that was for sure.

He watched the kid reach the entrance to the shelter.

Watched him kick back against the door.

Watched him pull that woman's limp body inside.

He climbed up onto the platform.

Walked over to the door as the kid slammed it shut.

As he fumbled around with something on the other side.

And then backed away.

Carlton walked up to the door.

Went to push it.

It wouldn't budge.

He stood there in the rain. Stared into the shelter. Stared at the boy, who stared back at him.

He smiled.

He wasn't going anywhere any time soon.

He was in no rush here.

No rush at all.

It was time to have some fun.

CHAPTER THIRTEEN

Billy shoved the long, loose piece of metal behind the door handles and backed away.

He was panting. Exhausted. His whole body was shaking. He was freezing cold, covered in rain, finally sheltered—only not sheltered that well because he could hear rain falling in through a hole in the room somewhere above.

But as he tried to catch his breath, there was only one thing he could focus on.

The man.

The man standing at the door.

Right at the glass.

Looking in at him.

Staring.

Smiling.

Billy stayed still. Totally still. He didn't have a choice. He couldn't move.

He was like a rabbit in the headlights, and he knew it.

This man. Standing here. He looked so calm. He looked so... happy.

He stared at Billy without saying anything. Just looked at him.

And Billy wondered if maybe he was in his mind. If maybe he wasn't real. And in a way, that made it scarier. Because he looked real. And if he wasn't real... he knew he wouldn't be able to sleep at night knowing how close this man was.

But then the man reached for the handle of the doors.

Rattled it. Tried to open it. Tried to shake it free.

Billy felt a wet patch forming in his jeans, and he felt guilty about it right away. Stopped himself. He used to get told off by Ramiro's people for that. Although some of them seemed to like it.

"Please, Aoife," he said. "Please."

He looked down at her. He was shaking. He'd only just managed to drag her in here. She was still out like a light.

He needed her to wake up. Because they couldn't stay here. He'd brought her in here for shelter, but they couldn't stay here because this man. He was banging at the door. He was going to get in.

Billy looked up again.

The man stared right at him. He looked scary. Like there was something just not right about him. Something *off* about him. Like he was a monster or an alien.

He didn't look like the man Aoife killed yesterday. The man on the road. He didn't look *mad* in that way.

But there was just something about him that made Billy feel so uncomfortable and scared.

"Please, Aoife," he said, crouching down, shaking her, trying desperately to get her to wake up. "Please!"

He listened to the rattling door.

His heart raced.

He shook everywhere.

"Please."

And then it stopped.

The door stopped rattling.

No more sounds.

Nothing.

He didn't want to look up. He didn't want to see. The door had stopped rattling. Which meant he had to be inside. He must've broken in.

He didn't *want* to look, but he knew he had to.

He lifted his head.

Slowly.

Shaking.

Heart racing.

Butterflies fluttering all around his tummy and chest.

Please. Please. Wake up, Aoife. Please.

When he looked up, he noticed something.

The man wasn't inside.

The man was gone.

He stayed there. Stayed totally still for longer. He had no idea how long. He didn't think it was possible, but he felt even more scared now he couldn't see the man.

The windows.

The windows all around this shelter.

He felt like a lion in a cage at a zoo.

Like he was being watched.

"B... Billy?"

Billy looked down.

Aoife was awake. Squinting. She looked confused.

"Aoife," he said. "You—you—we need to—"

"What... what happened..."

"I—We got caught out there. I had to... I had to get you in here. Aoife, listen. Please listen. There's—there's someone out there. A man. He... I'm scared, Aoife. I'm scared."

Aoife sat up. She didn't look fully with it. Her nose was still breathing, and she was still squinting. "You don't... you don't have to worry about anyone anymore."

"No, you don't understand. There's—there's a man. He was—

he was trying to break in here. Trying to get me. Trying to get both of us."

Aoife stood up. Unsteady on her feet. She staggered over towards the door.

"Aoife," Billy said. "Be careful. He's—"

"I don't see anyone," she said. Standing right at the door. Right at the glass. "There's nobody here, Billy. See?"

He shook his head. He didn't want to walk over to the door.

Because he was scared of finding someone?

Or because he was worried about what it meant if he didn't?

"Billy," Aoife said. "I know you're scared. And I know we've... I know a lot of shit's gone down. But it's okay now. Whoever was here... they're gone. See?"

Billy didn't want to walk over to Aoife's side, over to that window.

But he knew he had to.

He walked over. Slowly. Looking outside at all times. Just in case that man appeared again.

Because he was out there.

He *had* to be out there.

"We're okay now. Whoever... whoever was here, they aren't here anymore. See?"

He walked over to the glass.

Suddenly, a bang.

He jumped back and screamed.

Aoife laughed.

Billy shook his head. "What's..."

And then he saw it, right there on the glass.

A crow sliding down the window.

"It's fine," Aoife said. "Just a bird. Dumb thing survived this long, and it goes and flies itself into a window."

She laughed again. Shook her head.

All Billy could do was stare outside.

Stare out at the fact Aoife was right. Nobody was here.

Watch that crow slide down the window and hit the ground in a heap.

"We're okay," Aoife said. "It's gonna be okay."

Billy wanted to believe her.

But he couldn't get that man's stare and his smile out of his mind.

CHAPTER FOURTEEN

"You okay?" Aoife asked.

Billy stared at the train tracks. He hadn't said a lot since they'd left the shelter at the last stop earlier. He kept on looking back, then looking around.

"Seriously, kid," Aoife said. "It's okay. He's gone. Just a looney from the sounds of things. You don't have anything to worry about. Not anymore."

Billy looked up at her. But he looked concerned. Didn't have that confidence about him she'd seen for the rest of her time with him, especially after escaping Ramiro. He looked worried again.

"There was something about him," Billy said. "Something... bad."

Aoife nodded. She didn't want to disregard the lad. After all, she knew gut feelings could go a long way.

She looked back. The storm had eased and the skies had cleared again. Actually quite nice now. Bright. Amazing how quickly things could change. God, she was so British. Spent far too much time thinking about the weather. A hallmark of small talk if ever she needed it again.

"I hear you," she said. "But you saw what I saw. The shelter.

He wasn't there. He's nowhere. He's gone. We don't have to worry about him anymore. And besides. We've got weapons. We've got knives. It's not like we can't defend ourselves. Right?"

Billy nodded. But again, he didn't look entirely convinced. Something about this man he'd run into had seriously bothered him. Got under his skin.

"How're you anyway?" Billy asked.

"Oh, me? I'm doing just fine, thanks for asking."

"You got thrown a long way. Banged your head bad. Nose keeps bleeding. And you don't look..."

"Don't look what?"

"I don't know," Billy said. "But you've looked better."

Aoife laughed a little. "Charming. Definitely don't go saying that to the ladies of Rhyl."

"I don't..."

"What?"

Billy shook his head. "Nothing."

They walked further down the tracks. They'd have to turn off them eventually, but for now, they were safe heading in this direction. It was going to be a long and monotonous journey. And aside from the storm and the creepy bloke so far, things were going... relatively well.

But that wasn't entirely true, was it? Because Aoife felt like shit. She was shaky. Seriously shaky. Felt like she could collapse again at any second. Kept seeing these flashes and these floaters in her vision, blocking her view for a split second before disappearing again.

Her head was aching. She was shivery. She could taste blood. And she kept getting these shooting pains in her chest and stomach. Maybe she still had a bit of fucking lightning inside her.

"What are the odds?" Aoife said.

"Huh?"

"Struck by lightning. I can't remember what the odds are. But it's definitely not an everyday occurrence."

"They were probably punishing you for that Freddo pun before."

"Hey," Aoife said. "It was you who were making those stinkers, I think you'll find."

Billy laughed. It was good to see him smiling again. Especially what'd happened back there.

And then she felt another of those shooting pains.

Stopped in her tracks. Clutched her chest. Just for a second. Felt like her heart was skipping a beat.

"You okay?" Billy asked.

No. No, I'm not okay. I'm not okay, and this isn't good, and I need to get you as close to Rhyl as possible because…

No. She couldn't think that way.

"I will be," Aoife said. "Just been through the wars these last few days, hmm?"

Billy didn't look convinced. But he nodded. "Right."

"Right. Now come on. Let's keep moving."

Billy looked back. Then looked around. He visibly swallowed a lump in his throat, then turned around and carried on walking.

Aoife looked back, too.

She looked down the tracks. At the grass verges either side. At the trees surrounding them.

For a moment, for just a split second, she swore she saw a figure standing there between the trees.

Watching.

CHAPTER FIFTEEN

Carlton stood between the trees and watched "Billy" and "Aoife" walk down those tracks.

Billy. Billy. He kept on rolling that name through his mind. He'd heard the woman, Aoife, say it. And he'd heard him say her name.

And it made the pair of them more *real* somehow. It made him long even more for that boy.

Just knowing his name made the whole chase all the more... tantalising.

He was annoyed the woman, Aoife, had woken up. He had to admit that. He'd disappeared and climbed atop the shelter. Looked down through the opening in the roof, down at Billy standing there over that woman. Fear on his face. Fear, as he looked around and realised that Carlton was gone.

And then the woman woke up.

She went and woke up, and it ruined things. Because he wanted to get to that boy. He wanted to take Billy somewhere. He wanted it to just be the pair of them. The woman, she was just a complication. She was just going to get in the way.

But on the other hand... at least it meant this hunt was going to stretch on for even longer.

And that brought a sense of satisfaction in itself.

He saw Billy look around, look right up towards him. For a moment, he swore he looked right into his eyes. Fully expected him to say something to Aoife. To alert her to his presence.

But he just turned around and kept on walking.

The pair of them just kept on walking.

Carlton sighed. Smiled. Shook his head. He was just being paranoid. No way would the boy see him all this way away. No way would *anyone* see him all this way away.

But he could do with a little fate working in his favour, that was for sure.

He looked up at the sun. The clear sky. No sign of storms anymore. He'd missed the boat. That storm had really held the pair of them up.

But there was another problem.

A problem he could see clearly. Didn't take a genius.

The woman was struggling.

Aoife was struggling.

She was limping. And she was unsteady on her feet. Clearly trying her best to look stable but not doing a very good job. Not to Carlton, anyway.

He looked at the woman, and in all truth, he had no real feelings about her. Once upon a time, he might've been compelled to involve her in his plans.

But now...

The boy was far more interesting to him.

He watched them walk further down the tracks. Up ahead, he could see rubble. He knew they were going to get slowed down there. Knew they were going to run into trouble. And maybe he could get that to work in his favour.

He clenched his fists. Tasted blood. Realised he was biting his cheeks. Hard.

He got a little kick from the taste of blood. Got a little buzz from it.

Nothing compared to the real thing.

And he was going to get that real thing.

He was going to get it very soon.

He watched the pair of them get further along those tracks, and he took a deep breath.

Then, he walked down the slope, out from the security of the trees, and onto the tracks.

It was time to step things up a notch.

CHAPTER SIXTEEN

Billy couldn't stop looking around, over his shoulder, because he felt like someone was watching.

Felt like that man was watching.

He looked back at the trees. Looked down the tracks. Every little movement made him jump. A bird flying by. A fox running across the tracks. And then Aoife would say something or make a noise, and that would make him jump even more.

He just couldn't get that man out of his mind.

He'd seen him. He knew he'd seen him. He knew it wasn't in his head. And as much as Aoife told him not to worry and told him he was gone... he didn't believe her.

He'd seen that look in his eyes, and he knew there was something different about this man.

"We're gonna have a problem here, Billy."

Billy turned around. He'd been so focused on looking around that he hadn't thought to look ahead for a while.

Aoife stood beside him. She looked pale. Shaky. She didn't look well. And she wasn't saying much, either. It was like she was trying to hide how she really felt from Billy because she was worried about scaring him—and in a way that just scared him even more.

"What?" he said.

Aoife nodded ahead. "See for yourself."

Billy looked around, and his stomach sank.

There was a train right across the tracks. It was on its side, completely blocking their way. Windows were smashed. It was going all rusty. It'd been there a long time.

And as he looked closer, he realised it wasn't just one train. It was two.

"We're gonna struggle getting through here," Aoife said.

The butterflies in Billy's stomach fluttered even harder. "We—we could climb through. It doesn't look so bad."

"Or we could climb the slopes at the side here and go around it. Longer route. Those slopes look muddy as hell. Lots of loose branches and trees, too. But it might be safer."

Billy looked up at the slope at his side. He looked at those dead trees all across it. It was going to be even harder getting up there, and it would take a lot longer.

"I know what you're thinking," Aoife said. "But it's definitely safer that way. Nothing's less safe than something man-made."

"But..."

"But what?"

Billy looked back. Down the tracks. At the thicker trees either side. And he couldn't shake that feeling he was still being watched.

"Billy."

"I just... Something doesn't feel right."

Aoife sighed. He could tell she was getting irritable with him. Probably because she felt so rough. But if she'd seen what he had... he was pretty sure she'd be thinking the same thing.

"I—I know what I saw back there. And I... I just want to get through this as quick as possible."

"You must have a death wish, kid. Seriously. The amount of situations you've found yourself in and still you haven't learned."

"That's... that's not a nice thing to say."

A pause. Another sigh. "No. You're right. It's not. I'm sorry. But we're not getting anywhere by standing here. And... and sometimes, kiddo, you're just going to have to trust me. We're not going through that train. We're going to climb. If we're struggling, then we can try a plan B. But unless you want to split up, which absolutely isn't happening, this is how we're going to do things. Okay?"

Billy shook his head. He wasn't happy about this.

But at the same time, he didn't like the idea of being separated from Aoife.

And besides. What was he so worried about?

He looked around again. Right down the tracks.

Then back up at the trees.

He took a deep breath.

It's okay. He's not here. It's just like Aoife said. He's gone.

"As long as we can get moving one way or another and stop standing here, I'm in."

"Okay," Billy said.

Aoife sighed a breath of relief. "That's more like it."

They walked over to the slope at the side of the train tracks. The closer they got to it, the more awkward Billy thought it looked. Loads of branches everywhere. Branches he was going to have to hold on for support because the grass was so muddy and slippery.

"Come on," Aoife said, grabbing a few of the branches and dragging herself up. "It's fine, see?"

She almost slipped over when she said, "fine". Which made Billy laugh a little.

"Hey," she said, narrowing her eyes. "Don't you smirk like that. I'll be the one smirking here when we get up this slope in one piece."

Billy nodded. Laughed a little. He felt a bit more at ease now, even though he was worried about this. Worried about the man. Worried about that feeling he had of being watched.

He dragged himself up the slope. His feet slipped down right away as he tumbled to the mud. But he kept holding on like this was just some sort of adventure course.

He could do this.

He looked around at Aoife. Saw her arms shaking as she tried to grip on. She was breathing heavily. Sounded and looked like she was really struggling.

"Sure you don't want to change your mind?" Billy asked as he raced past her, getting into this now.

Aoife looked at him. Bloodshot eyes. She looked bad. Really bad. And her nose was bleeding again. "Let's just... let's just get to the top before we start boasting, okay?"

Billy would tease her more. But she looked like she was struggling.

He looked around, and he felt strong. Felt stronger than he'd ever felt. Everything his dad said about him not being strong enough or sporty enough. Everything the other kids teased him about.

And he was still here.

He was alive.

And he was...

"Billy! Watch out!"

He heard Aoife's voice and looked at her.

Saw the panic in her eyes as she stared up.

"What..."

He looked around and saw something hurtling down the slope towards him.

"How..."

And then he felt whatever it was slam into him and send him flying back down the slope.

CHAPTER SEVENTEEN

It all happened so fast.

One second, Aoife saw Billy clambering past her, working his way up the slope, moving between the branches with confidence, and she couldn't help feeling a twinge of jealousy because she was having a very bloody hard time about it. Felt weak. Felt rough. Felt like total shit.

And then the next...

She saw something. Right up above. Something at the top of the slope.

She didn't see who was behind it. And she couldn't make sense of it. Not at first.

But something was rolling down the slope.

Rolling towards her.

"Billy! Watch out!"

But it was too late.

Whatever was hurtling down the slope twisted. Turned, so it wasn't heading towards her; it was heading towards Billy instead.

"Watch out!"

She let go of the branch to try and push him out of the way.

But she just slipped.

Slipped down the muddy slope.

And then she heard whatever it was slamming against Billy and knocking the wind from his lungs—rather audibly.

She saw him tumbling down the slope with whatever it was that'd hit him. She watched him falling, picking up in speed, like a snowball, and she felt guilty. Because she'd made him come this way. She'd been the one to pick this route.

"Billy!"

She didn't even think about herself anymore.

She just let go of the loose grip she had on the branches and tumbled down after Billy.

She watched him fall as she slid down in the mud. Felt branches slamming against her face, scratching her as she slid by. She didn't think it would be possible to feel even weaker and like she'd been through the shit any more than she already did. But she did.

"Come on," she muttered. "Please. Please."

She fell to the bottom of the slope, and then she rolled over. Hit the tracks with a thud, cracking right against the solid ground. She winced. She felt so frail. This must be what age felt like. Aching everywhere. Like she'd been through a bunch of rounds with a pro boxer.

She lay there on the tracks and opened her eyes.

She looked up, up towards the top of the slope. Colours filling her vision. Lights flashing in her eyes. Ears ringing.

And up there, right at the top, as she lay there feeling more and more faint, she swore she saw something.

Or some*one*.

A man.

A man standing there.

Hands on his hips.

Looking down the slope.

She blinked. Tried to pull herself forward. Billy. She had to check on Billy. She had to make sure he was okay.

"Billy," she gasped. She could taste blood, strong in the back of her throat and her nostrils. She looked around, unbalanced, struggling to focus.

And then she saw him.

He was lying there beside her.

He was still.

And there was a bloody mark on his head.

"Billy," Aoife said. "I..."

And then she saw him move.

He looked around at her.

Sat up.

Wincing a little.

Wiping tears from his eyes.

"Are you okay?" Aoife asked.

Billy rubbed the back of his head. Pulled his hand out. There was blood on his fingers. "Banged my head. Hard. What..."

"I don't know," Aoife said, looking back up the slope. "But I saw..."

There was nobody up there anymore.

No man standing there, looking down.

"You saw him," Billy said. "Didn't you?"

Aoife didn't say anything. She just stared up at the top of that slope, feeling a little steadier now. A little more in control. Emphasis on the "a little".

"Whatever I saw, it's... I think maybe we should try the tracks."

Billy didn't say anything. He didn't have to. The way he looked at her, blood on his fingers, and on his head... that said enough.

"Yeah, yeah," Aoife said. "No need to look at me like that. Whatever happened just now we didn't know about. It was still the best thing to do."

Billy shrugged. Didn't say anything. He was clearly milking this. At least he was okay. If he wanted to be smug, then she'd just have to suck it up.

"Come on," she said. Shivering. Feeling freaked out about the whole thing. Not to mention absolutely knackered. "We need to..."

And then she stopped.

She saw something on the tracks.

Something right between her and Billy.

"This is what they pushed down the slope," Billy said. "This... this is what they threw at us."

Aoife stared at the thing lying in front of her, and she knew right away that Billy was right.

They weren't just dealing with something trivial here.

They were dealing with someone very, very disturbed.

It was a body.

A body of a man.

He looked alarmingly overweight for someone who'd clearly survived a long time in this powerless world. Didn't look like starvation had ever been a problem. Not exactly the healthiest looking guy. But Aoife had seen far worse.

But it was the state of him that really caught her eye.

Or rather, *his* eyes that really caught her eye.

There were bloody holes where they once were.

Tears of blood ran down this man's cheeks.

And that blood looked fresh.

A scream was etched on this man's dead mouth as he stared blankly up into the bright blue sky.

"It's him," Billy said. Staring down at the body. "He did this."

"We don't know that—"

"He did this."

Aoife went to argue. But there was nothing she could say. Nothing she could prove or disprove.

She just knew they needed to keep moving.

She wanted to get the hell away from here. Fast.

"Come on," she said, looking down at that body, barely able to take her eyes from it. "Let's... let's get moving."

Billy looked at the body. Then over at the train tracks and the slopes either side.

And then he followed Aoife, down the tracks, towards that train wreckage.

Aoife couldn't stop thinking about that man's terrified stare as he lay there, eyeless.

And she couldn't shake the feeling that someone was watching.

CHAPTER EIGHTEEN

arlton watched Aoife and Billy walk towards the train wreckage, and he smiled.

He'd been lucky. Very fucking lucky. First, lucky enough to find that fat bloke lying dead by the side of the road beside the train tracks. Looked like he'd run into some trouble. Relatively recently, too.

Eyes cut out. Stabbed away.

The kind of method he would enjoy.

Only he wasn't responsible.

Someone else out there had done it.

He'd looked around when he'd found the man's body. Then he'd dragged him over to the side of the slope. Originally, he'd planned on just leaving him lying around to spook Aoife and Billy into going where he wanted them to go.

But when he saw them climbing the slope... he had another idea.

A chance to get rid of the woman.

Especially with her looking so weak.

So he'd stood at the side of that slope, made sure he was

crouched from view, and he'd pushed. Pushed the body over the side of the slope, lining it up perfectly so it'd go tumbling down towards Aoife.

Only it'd turned direction as it fell. The fat bastard changed his path, started snowballing towards Billy instead.

And Carlton could only watch with his breath held as it slammed into Billy.

As it knocked him down the slope.

As he slammed back onto the tracks, still for a scary few seconds.

Only to see Billy stand again.

To see Aoife stand.

He saw her looking up at him, the woman, when she woke. And he enjoyed that. Because that sense of fear. They would be fully aware he was still following them now. Which meant he had to be more careful, of course.

But this was all part of the thrill. If Billy died when he'd pushed that fat shit's body over the slope, it would take all the fun of the chase out of things. He'd be back to square one.

And his hunger wasn't getting weaker any time soon...

He watched them both walk by. Aoife and Billy. And there was something about their resilience and togetherness that he admired. And he started to wonder if maybe they *would* be fun to hunt as part of a package deal, after all. Sure, a kid was new territory for him. And sure, maybe he should build up to double-murder. Didn't want to burn out on children by jumping ahead and going for something more taboo too soon.

But hell. He'd travelled a long way. And he'd been relatively bereft of killings lately.

Maybe he would treat himself.

Maybe he would indulge.

He watched the pair of them stop right in front of that abandoned train wreckage.

He smiled.

He knew exactly what he had to do next.

He took a deep breath, and he walked away.

It was time for them to come face to face with one another.

It was time to up the stakes.

It was time to take this beautiful hunt to a whole new level.

CHAPTER NINETEEN

"You still sure this is such a good idea, Billy?"

Billy looked at the train wreckage ahead, and he felt nervous. It'd been here a long time. All the windows were smashed. It looked like plants had started growing up the side of it. There was glass everywhere.

And it sounded creaky. Very creaky.

He looked around. Back down the train tracks. He couldn't see anyone here. And then up to the slopes either side of the tracks.

"I guess... I guess there's no other way," he said.

"You don't sound quite as sure about going this way anymore," Aoife said.

Billy didn't say anything. He just wished Aoife would stop bringing that up. He knew he'd wanted to go this way at first because it looked like the quicker way to go, and he wanted to get as far away from that man as he could.

But now he was here... he couldn't even see the other side properly. He didn't know how they were going to get through it. Whether they were going to go over, or under, or inside.

But they needed to do something.

That body.

The one that knocked him down the slope.

He kept on thinking of it every time he felt a pain inside.

That had to be the man.

He'd done something to that body, and he was toying with Billy and Aoife.

Why?

He had no idea. But they had to get away.

"We could go under it," Billy said.

Aoife shrugged. Crouched down. "It looks pretty blocked at the other side to me."

"Then what do you think we should do?"

She walked over to the bottom of the train, which faced them. Grabbed it and pulled herself up onto it. Wincing. Struggling. Clearly not as strong as she once was.

But when she was up there, she turned around. Billy heard the train creak as she looked at him and held her hands out. "Come on. All or nothing here. Get a move on."

He looked over his shoulder again.

Then he walked over to her.

Reached for her hands.

Climbed up the side of the train.

Aoife wobbled. Struggled to hold her footing. Which worried Billy even more. Because he thought he might fall and drag her down with him.

But then he got onto the side of the train. Stood there with her. Watched her gasping. Holding her chest. Wincing.

"You okay?"

"I'm fine."

"But you—"

"I'm fine, Billy. Just... come on. We need to go."

He knew she didn't look good. She looked terrible.

But he didn't want to say anything else to her right now.

She walked over to the large window at the side of the train.

Looked ahead. The wreckage of the next train completely blocked their way ahead. There was no way they could climb this one, either. Or if they did, it would be dangerous. Very dangerous.

"We drop down into this train," Aoife said. "We work our way through it. Slowly. Carefully. We get to the other side."

"And then?"

"And then, Billy, we pray."

Billy wasn't sure it sounded like a great plan. But it was the only plan they had. Damn it. Things seemed so good when he was climbing that slope before. He felt confident. He felt on top of the world.

But now he felt scared again. Now, he felt unsure.

"We'll be okay," he said. "Won't we?"

Aoife looked at him. Didn't answer for a bit too long.

But then she forced a smile and nodded. "We'll have to be. Now come on. After me."

She stepped into the opening where the window was.

Disappeared into the darkness of the train below.

Billy looked around.

Still nobody on the train tracks.

Still nobody around at all.

"It'll be fine," he said. "He's gone now. It'll be okay."

"Billy?"

Billy looked around. Saw Aoife standing inside that dark train.

"Come on," she said. "We've got to get moving."

Billy took a deep breath.

Then he stepped down into the remains of the train.

This train was completely different to the one they'd slept in last night. It was darker. Dirtier. He could see things scuttling around everywhere—rats and bugs. Pigeon shit all over the place.

The smell was strong. Sour. Rotten.

And the seats were filled with bodies.

Well, skeletons.

Some were more like skeletons than others. Some still had weird grey skin.

But there were lots of them.

So many of them who had died in this train accident.

People who hadn't even known about the blackout.

They were lucky, in a way. They'd died right when the world had its last good moment.

"Come on," Aoife said.

She walked ahead, and Billy followed closely behind. He tried not to look at those skeletons, but he couldn't help himself. They were covered in cobwebs. Big spiders crawling across them.

Just look ahead, Billy. Just look ahead.

He followed Aoife further down through this dark train. It got tighter. And the ground got uneven. And Billy realised he was walking across rotting bodies and bones.

The eyes of rats staring back at him from the corner.

"Just a little further," Aoife said. "We should be able to get through here."

Billy took another few steps and heard the train creak. He looked around, back the way they'd come from.

Nothing.

Nobody here.

Heart beating faster and faster.

"This is it," Aoife said. "Through here."

Billy stopped right beside her and saw it.

A window. Partly broken.

But leading out onto the ground below.

"How... What..."

"We need to climb out of here," Aoife said. "And then... and then climb under the next train."

Billy swallowed a lump in his throat. "I can't—"

"Now's not the time to be claustrophobic, Billy. We need to get a move on. Come on."

"You... I don't want to go first."

"You have to go first. So I can watch you. And if anything... if anything happens to me. I..."

She stopped. She didn't want to say it, but Billy knew what she was getting at.

She wasn't well.

If something happened to her down there, he'd be trapped.

But still...

"I... I don't want to go first. And I know it's bad. And selfish. But I... I'm sorry. I'm just scared."

Aoife walked over to him. Put a hand on his shoulder.

"No," she said. "Of course. I'm sorry. Okay. I'll go first. But just... just stay close, okay? And if anything happens..."

She didn't finish what she was saying.

She didn't have to.

She turned around and climbed out of the window.

"Thank you," Billy said.

Aoife stopped. Just for a second. Looked back at him.

"Thank me when we get to the other side."

She disappeared out through that window.

Squeezed her way outside.

Billy heard another creak.

Looked back.

Still nobody there.

Just the wind. That's all it was.

"Shit," Aoife said.

"What?"

"It's... it's tighter than I thought."

Billy's heartbeat picked up.

"There's no coming back," Aoife said. "Once you're down here. So we're going to have to make a break for it. Okay?"

Billy nodded. Getting more and more scared. But knowing it's what he had to do. "Okay."

"Now, Billy," she said. "Follow me."

He stepped over the opening.

Looked down into the darkness.

You're strong.

You don't have to worry about the monsters in the dark anymore.

You're going to be okay.

He went to lower himself down through that opening when he heard another creak.

He turned around.

And when he looked back, his entire body froze.

The man stood at the top of the train.

Looking right down the length of the carriage at him.

Smiling.

CHAPTER TWENTY

Billy saw the man standing there at the top of the train, and he froze.

Time stood still. He felt fear. Total fear. He could hear Aoife saying things to him. Maybe he was saying things to her, too. He couldn't tell.

He was just lost, and he was afraid.

The man stood there with that smile on his face. With that flicker in his eyes.

And he stood still.

Very still.

Like he was waiting for Billy to do something.

Waiting for him to make a move.

"Billy? What the hell's wrong up there?"

"He's... he's here," Billy said. But it was quiet. Far too quiet for anyone to hear him.

"What? Hurry up. You're starting to freak me out."

"He's here," he said. Louder this time. "The man. He's here."

Aoife didn't say anything back. Not for a moment.

The man stayed there. Still. Very still.

"Get down here," Aoife said. "Get down here right this second."

Billy turned to the window and went to jump down.

And right on cue, the man marched down the carriage towards him.

Billy dropped down below. Shaking. It was tight down here. The train was almost touching the ground. Up ahead, in the darkness, he could see Aoife. The metal from the train pressing against her. Light at the other side. If this train shifted just a little bit, they would suffocate.

"Billy," Aoife said. "Come on. Now!"

She started dragging herself along because the only way for Billy to move was for Aoife to move, too.

And he could hear those footsteps getting louder above him.

He could hear them getting closer.

Aoife dragged herself along, and as she did, Billy did too.

He just had to keep moving.

He just had to get away from that opening.

He just had to—

A hand.

A hand grabbing his ankle.

Yanking him back.

"Aoife!"

"Billy!"

He tried to hold onto the train. Tried to hold onto the ground. But it was no use.

The man was dragging him back towards that train.

He looked into Aoife's eyes as he jolted further back, and he knew he had to reach for his knife—but his knife was out of reach, and he didn't have time.

He felt glass.

A sharp shard from a window, right by his fingers, nicking him. He grabbed it.

And then he turned onto his back and swung it at that man's arm.

Hard.

The man let out a cry.

Loosened his grip on Billy's ankle.

And Billy kicked back at him.

Kicked back and then scrambled forward again, towards Aoife, towards that opening, towards their way out of here.

"Come on," Aoife said, still moving. "You're—you're going to do this. You've got this. You're doing great."

He clambered his way between that narrow opening, the only opening in this wreckage. An opening just about big enough to fit one person through at a time. The wreckage above kept on creaking. Sounded like it could collapse at any moment.

But he had to keep going.

He dragged himself along. He could hear the man wincing, cursing. The first words he'd heard him say.

But as long as he kept on going, he'd be okay here.

He dragged himself further and further and realised Aoife had stopped.

"Aoife?"

Aoife looked around at him. Her nostrils were bleeding again. Come to think of it... so too were her eyes.

"Aoife, no," Billy said. "We—we need to keep going. Like you said."

Aoife nodded. Then she stretched an arm out in front of her. Tried to pull herself further along.

"Please," Billy said. "Don't... Not now. Not now."

Aoife opened her mouth like she was going to say something.

Then her eyes rolled back into her skull, and she collapsed and started fitting, right there on the ground, right in front of Billy.

He lay there. Lay on his stomach.

Aoife before him. Suffering. Badly.

And blocking his way past.

He looked back.

He didn't see the man there.

He didn't hear the man there.

He didn't see or hear anyone there.

Billy lay there on the ground. Loose glass digging into him. Train tracks digging into him.

He squeezed his eyes shut, held on to Aoife as she fitted, and he prayed.

"Please be okay," he said. "Please be okay."

But there was no getting around the mess he was in here.

He was trapped.

Aoife on one side.

And that man on the other.

And there was nothing he could do to get out.

CHAPTER TWENTY-ONE

Billy shook Aoife's body and tried to wake her up, but he was beginning to worry she wouldn't ever wake up again.

He could hear heavy rain hammering down on the train carriage above him. He was crying. Because he was stuck, and he didn't like being in enclosed spaces, and he was trapped, and he couldn't breathe, and he just wanted to be away from here.

Far, far away from here.

He held on to Aoife's body, shaking with cold, shaking with fear. "Wake up, Aoife. Please. Please, wake up."

She wasn't fitting anymore. She wasn't moving anymore. She was still. Totally still.

He tried to feel for a heartbeat, tried to see if she was breathing. But he couldn't properly tell. Every time he thought he felt something, he heard movement above. Creaking. The train carriage pressing against him as it moved in the wind.

And then there was the man.

The man who was after him. He hadn't seen him for a while. Not since he'd grabbed him and tried to drag him back inside the train.

Not since Billy stabbed him.

He'd gone quiet. Hadn't heard him for ages. Maybe he'd gone. Maybe he'd died. Maybe Billy had stabbed him harder than he thought.

Or maybe he was still in that train. Waiting.

Billy turned around to Aoife. Tried to wake her again. "Aoife, please. We need to go."

But it didn't matter what he did or said. Aoife wasn't moving.

Billy cried. He leaned against Aoife's body, and he cried. He was starting to trust her. She'd helped him. And now she was gone. Just like everyone else, she was gone.

He waited there a while before lifting his head, being careful not to bang it on the train above. He had to do something. He couldn't just stay here. As scared as he was, he would die under here if he waited here too long.

He owed it to Aoife to get out of here.

To carry on to Rhyl.

To find a new home.

He pushed against Aoife as hard as he could, feeling bad about it right away.

He didn't want to hurt her.

He didn't want her to be in any pain.

And he didn't want to even think about the possibility that she might be dead.

No. Don't think that. Don't think that.

But as he pushed against her with all his force, he knew it was the only thing he could do. There was no way around her, otherwise; it was too narrow down here. And there was no way over her, either. He didn't want to get stuck.

He pushed, dug his toes into the cold ground.

"Come on," he said, trying to force her along. Every inch of his body in agony as he tried. "Come on!"

But she wasn't moving.

He just wasn't strong enough to shift her down here.

He gave up. Lay flat on his stomach. He wondered how long

he could last down here, alone. He wondered just how long it'd be before that man came down here and tried to grab him. Or gave up and disappeared.

He wondered how long he could survive down here.

Because something told Billy that man wasn't going away.

Something told him he wasn't going to give up.

He pushed against Aoife's weight again. Shifted her, just a little bit. And then he waited and gasped and panted and pushed her again, crying as he did it, unable to accept she was gone.

Because she couldn't be gone. Not just like that.

This couldn't be the end.

He pushed harder and harder until his arms were numb and shaky and he had absolutely no strength left in his body.

And then he stopped and fell face flat against the ground again.

He had to accept it as he lay there, heart racing. He had to face the truth.

He wasn't getting out of this.

He wasn't pushing Aoife out of the way.

He looked back. Over at that train. Over towards where he'd come from. Aoife said she couldn't turn around. But he was smaller, so he thought he probably could.

He listened. Still no sounds from that man. Still no idea whether he was even still here.

He looked around at Aoife, then. Shook his head.

"I'm sorry. I don't... I don't want to leave you. But I have to try something. I have to. Right?"

She didn't say a word in response.

He closed his stinging eyes, and he cried again. He hadn't felt this sad for a long time. Even with all the horrible things Ramiro and his people did to him... he'd not felt like this for ages.

"I'm sorry. But I'll... I'll come back to you. I'll find a way to come back to you. I won't... I won't let you get stuck under here forever. I'll make sure of it."

And then he reached over and kissed her on the head.

"Thank you. I'll come back for you. I promise I will."

He swore he heard her take a breath just as he turned around.

He wormed his way around. Tried to twist his body and turn, but the space was tight, and it was hard.

But eventually, he made it. He was facing backwards again.

Back towards the train.

Towards the opening.

"Here goes nothing."

He dragged himself along the way he'd come from. Above, he couldn't see through any of the windows. They were blacked out.

Skeletons stared down at him.

He pulled himself further across the ground.

Kept on going until he reached that opening.

He stopped. Stopped there for a second. Waited.

He could see blood on the metal of the train dripping down. Blood from where he'd stabbed the man.

He held his breath. Listened.

Couldn't hear anything.

"You can do this. Back through the train. Figure out the rest when you've made it."

He lifted himself up.

Up through that gap.

Saw the skeletons.

Saw the bodies.

Saw the darkness.

And then saw the light at the top of the train.

He just had to run down there and make it.

No sign of the man.

He could do this.

He closed his eyes.

Took a deep breath.

"I'll come back for you," he said.

And then he opened his eyes and pulled himself back onto the train.

He didn't stop to think.

He ran.

Ran as fast as he could.

Ran up the carriage.

Ran towards the opening.

He was going to make it.

He was so close.

He was...

And then, out of nowhere, one of the bodies moved.

His eyes opened.

And Billy realised exactly who it was.

Before he could stop himself, the man jumped out from the seat and wrestled him to the ground.

He held his bloodied hand to Billy's mouth. Looked down at him with manic, bloodshot eyes. Smiled.

"Hello, Billy. My name's Carlton. And for the next day or so, we're going to get to know each other very, very well."

CHAPTER TWENTY-TWO

Aoife opened her eyes and immediately felt a wave of panic.

She was on her back, and she could taste blood. Her body ached everywhere. Her back, her legs, her neck, her face. For a second, she had no idea where she was.

She lifted her head and banged it against something hard. Lay back down on the cold, hard ground and squinted ahead. Colours in her eyes, spiralling in her vision. Her headache getting stronger and stronger. Where the hell was she?

And then it hit.

All at once, it hit.

The train carriage.

Billy being dragged back by some man.

And then fending him off, and...

She didn't remember the rest. It was all a blur. All a complete haze.

But one thing was for sure.

She'd passed out.

She was still under the carriage.

"Billy?" she said.

He didn't respond. Which filled her with fear.

She tried to turn around, but she was aching all over. She tried to see, but those colours still filled her gaze.

"Billy," Aoife said. "Where... where are you?"

But again, nobody responded.

She twisted around and immediately felt a surge of pain in her chest. It was tight down here. It was tight, and it would be her coffin if she didn't do something fast.

She looked back and saw no sign of Billy.

No sign of that man.

She wondered if Billy had got past her. If he'd walked on. But then... no. There was no getting over her. Not in this small space.

There was only one way he could've gone.

Back towards the train.

She tried to twist around, but that just hurt her even more. She wasn't small enough to manoeuvre in this space. Her legs and her arms ached, and she could barely move without feeling exhausted or like passing out again.

But she had to try.

"Billy," she called.

But she knew her shouts fell on deaf ears. Because wherever Billy was, he wasn't here.

She lay there. Stared at the ground.

You've got to do this, Aoife. You've got to at least fucking try.

She couldn't afford to mope around.

She couldn't afford to feel sorry for herself.

She had to act.

She held her breath and twisted herself around.

It was hard. And for one moment, she thought she might just break her back in the process.

But she kept on pushing.

Kept on turning...

And then she turned and fell forward, and she was facing the opening again.

"That's it," she said. "That's more like it. Come on."

She dragged herself along, shaking. If she got back fast, she could find Billy. She could stop that man taking him away or hurting him, whoever he was.

But she didn't even know how long she'd been out. She could hear it raining now. She didn't remember rain before.

She dragged her pained body further and further across the tracks until she reached the opening.

She dragged herself up into it.

Stood up.

In the darkness, panting, she saw no sign of life.

Just a hell of a lot of death.

"Billy!"

She walked up the aisle. Kept on going as she passed more and more bodies killed in this ancient train accident.

Until she reached the window she'd dropped through.

"Billy!"

She pulled herself onto the top—or the side—of the train.

Stood there on top of it.

She looked out at the train tracks.

At the slopes beyond.

At the hills in the distance where she and Billy came from.

And as she stood there, she saw no signs of life.

She saw no signs of Billy.

Or of anyone.

Billy was gone.

CHAPTER TWENTY-THREE

Aoife walked back down the road she'd come from.

It was raining heavily. Warmer now. Felt more like spring than winter. The skies were grey. It looked like another storm could be on the horizon.

She didn't care.

Billy was gone.

She limped down along the train tracks. She kept on looking around for signs of life. Signs that he was close. She looked for any trace of him—traces of footprints, traces of clothing, traces that he or that man he was so worried about had been here at all.

But there was nothing.

Nothing whatsoever.

She kept on walking. Her legs were heavy and weak. Her feet hurt. Her head throbbed. She felt dizzy. Like she needed something sugary to keep her awake. This constant taste loomed at the back of her throat.

She knew she'd passed out again. And based on how exhausted she felt... she wondered if she'd had another seizure. She didn't know why she was suddenly having these seizures. Probably a combination of the lightning strike and the beating she'd got from

Ramiro. It wasn't long ago. A matter of days. Felt like a lifetime ago.

Whatever the case, she wasn't well. And she had a terrifying realisation dawning on her that she wasn't ever going to make it off these tracks.

She was never going to find Billy.

She didn't have the strength to keep on going.

She tumbled down. Fell to her knees. A splitting pain in her chest, right around her heart, which hadn't stopped racing for a long while now. She closed her burning eyes and took deep breaths of that rainy air.

"Wherever you are," she said. "I'll find you. I made you a promise. I'll find you."

She opened her eyes, and she saw something up ahead.

It was only small. Barely noticeable. And it could be nothing.

But Aoife saw it the moment she opened her eyes, and she wondered.

It was bright. And it was shimmering in the sunlight, which barely broke through the clouds.

Blood.

She crouched down beside it. Touched it with her fingertips, then put her fingers to her tongue. Seemed fresh. Recent.

Which meant it could be Billy's.

Or it could be the man's.

Billy had stabbed him after all.

She lifted her head, squinted into the distance, and saw something else.

More specks of blood.

Leading down these tracks.

A path.

She stood up. Took a deep breath. Clenched her fists together.

She might be weak. She might be on death's door. She might not be able to push on much further.

But one thing was for sure.

She wasn't giving up on Billy.

Whether she found him at the end of this trail of blood or died trying, she wasn't giving up.

She took another deep breath.

And then she walked along the tracks, along the path of blood.

If she knew what she was walking towards, Aoife might've had second thoughts about it.

CHAPTER TWENTY-FOUR

Billy had no idea where he was, but he was afraid.

It was dark. He didn't know if he was blindfolded or not. Probably. He couldn't remember. He remembered the man, Carlton, jumping out at him on the train. He remembered him covering his mouth to stop him screaming and telling him they were going to get to know each other very well over the next day. Or was it week? He didn't know. He was scared, and he was confused, and now he was lost, and he had no idea where Aoife was or whether she was even alive still.

He was sitting down somewhere. His wrists were tied. Carlton had carried him for a long time. And Billy had watched as those train tracks passed by underneath him. He'd watched them walk right back the way they'd come from. Further and further and further away from Rhyl, from the place Aoife was supposed to be taking him to, that new home.

He must've drifted off at one point, watching the tracks pass by. Because now he was somewhere dark, blindfolded, cold.

And he had no idea where.

He looked around. Didn't see a thing in the darkness. His

wrists were tied together. His legs didn't feel tied, though, so maybe he could get up. Maybe he could walk.

He pushed back against the wall he was leaning against. Wiggled his way up it. He could smell dampness in the air. Hear water trickling down from above somewhere. A garage? Some kind of shed? He didn't know. Wasn't sure.

He just knew he needed to get out of here.

He reached for his blindfold, but his arms wouldn't reach, tied behind his back. He tried to rub his face against the wall and loosen the blindfold, but again, no luck.

He'd just have to work with what he had right now.

And what he had were his feet.

At least they were free.

He stayed still. Really still. Listened for breathing. Or for footsteps. Listened for any sign of life.

But he didn't hear a thing.

It made him nervous. Because wherever Carlton was, it didn't sound like he was right here. And in a way, that scared him even more. Because he didn't seem like the sort of man who'd just let him go. He seemed like the sort of man who'd really wanted Billy.

And now he was nowhere to be seen.

That was scary.

He tried to loosen his blindfold against the wall again. This time, he managed a little better. Saw a slight lightness outside it. Well, not lightness, but brighter than the dark of the blindfold anyway.

And it was something. He'd got the blindfold partly off. So now he just had to find out where he was and get out of here.

But the monsters are watching you, Billy...

He felt a surge of fear right away. Thought he saw movement in the darkness. Thought he saw things moving in the shadows. And they made him freeze. Made him totally still.

He couldn't move. He couldn't leave here.

Because the monsters were after him and...

Deep breath.

Deep, shaky breath.

"No," he muttered. "The monsters aren't real. You—you need to get out of here. You need to be strong."

He ignored the shimmering in the darkness and looked around. Felt the cold brick wall with his hands, which was damp and mossy. Felt like he was in some kind of garage, or old storage place, like where Dad used to take his car to get worked on. He wasn't sure, though.

He felt along the wall with his hands, which were behind him. But still he didn't find any doors, or any ways out, or anything like that.

He kept on looking. Kept on breathing. Tried to stay as calm as he could, even though he was so scared.

"You'll be okay. You'll find a way out. You'll..."

And then he felt it.

A handle.

A cold, metal handle.

The butterflies in his tummy flapped their wings harder.

He shuddered, with excitement, with fear.

"Come on. Almost there."

He started to turn the handle, which wasn't easy with his hands tied behind his back.

And then he stopped.

A noise.

A noise over at the other side of the room.

He peeked over, squinted into the darkness. His blindfold was falling back down. Soon, he wouldn't be able to see at all.

Movement in the darkness.

There was somebody here.

The man was here.

The monsters were here.

He was...

No.

Another deep breath.

He was going to be okay.

He was going to get out of this.

He wrapped his hands tighter around the handle. He knew it was probably locked. He knew it probably wouldn't open.

But he at least had to try.

He lowered the handle.

The door clicked open.

His eyes widened.

Light shone in. Moonlight. Dark outside.

But light.

A cold wind.

He was outside.

He'd made it.

As his blindfold slipped back over his face, as only a slither of vision worked its way in, he didn't even think anymore.

He didn't hesitate.

He stepped out of the door, and he ran.

He didn't know where he was running.

He didn't know where he was going.

But he ran as fast as he could and hoped and prayed.

He kept on going, and his hope started to rise.

He'd been running a while now, and he hadn't fallen, and nobody was trying to stop him.

He kept on running and running, and he started to feel hope again. He started to feel free again.

He was going to make it.

He was going to get away.

"I'm coming, Aoife," he said, tears streaming down his face. "I'm—"

"I don't think so."

He slammed into something.

Or someone.

Fell back.

Before he could fall, the person caught him.

His stomach sank. His body shook. Time stood still.

And then, out of nowhere, the man lifted his blindfold and smiled at him.

"You're not going anywhere, little one," Carlton said.

CHAPTER TWENTY-FIVE

Aoife followed the blood trail until she lost all trace of it entirely.

It was dark. She had no idea how long she'd been walking, but it had to be hours. She felt exhausted. The showdown with Ramiro and the assault by Jarrod seemed like it was a distant dream, now. Or a nightmare.

So much had happened in these last few days. Her life had changed in so many ways. From convincing herself she was travelling with Kayleigh and Rex, to finding Billy, to accepting Kayleigh and Rex weren't still here... so much had happened.

And where had it all got her?

Beaten. Battered. Broken. And more alone than ever before.

But would she change it for a thing?

No, she fucking wouldn't.

She'd formed a connection with Billy. She'd opened her arms and heart and let him in. And as much as that thought of connection terrified her, as much as it was exactly what she'd been resisting for so long... she was in too deep to do anything about it now.

She looked around for a trace of blood but couldn't find any.

Metal fences lined the sides of this part of the track. They could've climbed over those. Or they could've kept walking. Fuck, she didn't even know whether the blood trail she'd been following even *was* Billy's or that bloke's.

But what the hell else did she have to go on?

There was another problem, too. Not to keep banging on about how rough she felt, but... fuck, yeah, she felt really rough. Her vision kept drifting away. For what felt like a split second, she lost all her senses. Hard to explain, but one moment she'd see something she was walking up to a certain distance from her, and within the blink of an eye, she'd be past it.

She didn't know what was happening to herself. The headaches were getting worse. Probably a bleed on the brain or some shit like that. Made sense after the turmoil her body had been through.

"Hell, if you made it through sepsis, Max, then I'll damn well make it through this."

She started walking again when she noticed something over to her right.

A gap. A gap in the fence. Looked like the metal had been opened so someone could squeeze through.

It was a long shot. No guarantees that man had passed through here with Billy. But she didn't have much else to go on right now, so she owed it to herself to check.

She limped over to the fence, every step a chore when she suddenly heard something behind her.

She froze.

Spun around.

She'd heard voices. Voices and footsteps, she was absolutely sure of it.

She stayed still. Stared into the darkness. She'd heard someone talking. Or was it all in her head? She couldn't forget the fact that she'd been imagining things just days ago. Convincing herself Kayleigh and Rex were still alive and with her.

What was to say this wasn't in her head, too?

Especially since she was in a far worse state physically now?

She shook her head, turned back around. Limped over towards that fence again.

She had to keep focused.

She had to keep her shit together.

She walked over to the fence, over towards that opening. Crouched down beside it. Which she kind of regretted right away because the way she was aching right now, it wasn't gonna be easy standing again.

She looked out through it, at the darkness beyond. She could see a road filled with cars. A few buildings beyond that. Farmhouses, by the looks of things. Looked pretty rural.

She went to climb through it when she noticed something.

Blood.

A bloody handprint on the metal fencing.

Shit. She'd found the path again. They'd gone this way. That had to be the man's handprint.

He couldn't be much further ahead. Especially not with how fresh the blood was.

She needed to watch herself.

She needed to be careful.

Very, very careful.

"I'm coming, Billy," she said. "I won't let you down."

She went to climb through the opening between the fencing when she heard something behind her again.

Movement.

Shuffling.

Footsteps.

Laughter.

She looked back.

Couldn't see anybody.

But she wasn't alone. She knew that for a fact now.

And right now, she wasn't so keen on running into anybody.

She turned around and climbed through that fence.

It's all in your head. There's nobody here. Everything's gonna be okay...

She faced the road.

Faced the farmhouses.

Took a deep, nervous breath and walked across the road.

She was going to find Billy.

And she was going to make that fucker who'd taken him pay for what he'd done.

SHE DIDN'T SEE them watching her closely.

Waiting for the perfect moment.

CHAPTER TWENTY-SIX

Carlton watched the blood drip from his arm and couldn't believe the little bastard hurt him like that.

But you know what? At the same time, he kind of admired it. It showed guts. It showed courage.

He was going to have a lot more fun with the boy for that.

He was going to put him through hell for it.

He sat outside the farmhouse and looked at the wooden door. Moonlight shone down bright from above. It didn't feel as cold tonight. Maybe that's just because he was enjoying the hunt. Getting closer and closer to the kill.

The anticipation was electric.

Billy had done well to escape as quickly as he had. Of course, that was all part of the plan. He wanted to give Billy hope. He wanted him to feel for one moment that he might actually stand a chance of getting away.

So he'd let him.

Let him run.

Let him keep on running with that blindfold wrapped around his eyes.

Smiled as he saw Billy crying and smirking, muttering to

himself about how he would make it, how he was going to be okay.

Really heart-warming stuff, truly.

But at the end of the day, he'd had to step in and stop him. He couldn't have him running too far away. Couldn't have him straying and basking in too much hope. Maybe that would come later. Maybe he'd let him feel like he really had escaped. Maybe he could stalk him again, for a few days this time.

Something about this boy was different. He didn't feel as compelled to kill him. Like, of course, he *was* going to kill him, eventually. And sure. The chase and the hunt were always exciting. He never felt fully satiated if he hadn't had at least a little while to luxuriate in anticipation.

But this boy, Billy... he had opened a whole world of new possibilities for Carlton. He felt like he could get high off the repeated snatching of hope, the same high he got from the killings.

And that felt... well. Unusual. It threw him into something of a quandary.

That rival voice in his head. He didn't like to listen to the one because it was weak and nonsensical.

What if he's the key?

Carlton shook his head. Bit down on his nails, which tasted of blood. Then he looked back at his arm, blood still trickling out. The boy had got him good. Again, it made him admire him even more. He had guts about him. Not a lot of people would have the courage to stand up to him like that, especially not a kid.

What if he's the key to making you better?

"I don't need to feel fucking better," Carlton snapped.

His head was spinning. He was growing dizzy. Weak. These voices in his head were getting louder.

And they were posing questions he didn't want to consider.

Maybe you don't have to kill him.

"I always have to kill. It's what keeps me going."

But maybe he can be different...

"No!"

He stuffed his fingers into the stab wound right on cue. Felt the pain surge through his body, completely dulling every single one of his senses.

And he felt better for that.

It shut the voice in his head up.

Because that voice in his head *needed* to shut the fuck up.

He couldn't go letting it give him any dangerous ideas.

But the idea's already there. He's different. You know that already. And if he weren't, you'd have killed him by now already.

"No!"

He stuck his fingers even further into the open wound. Hot blood poured out everywhere. He was starting to feel dizzy and sick. If he wasn't careful, that wound would get infected, and if you got infected in this world, you were as good as dead already.

He pulled his fingers away. Cried. The pain was the same as when he was a child. Exactly the same as what his dad used to do to him.

Those wounds on his arms.

The way he'd tell them they needed seeing to.

The way Dad would open them up.

Pour that burning alcohol on them.

Then close them up again with stitches.

Then open them before they could heal, and begin the cycle again, and again, and again...

And in a moment of rare self-reflection, in a moment of rare self-pity—because what did he have to pity? He had a perfect, honest life. He was living in tune with his desires. The same couldn't be said for anyone else.

But in that rare moment, he had one thought: no wonder he'd ended up on this path. No wonder he'd turned out just as messed up as his dad.

Maybe you don't have *to follow the same path...*

It was that thought which spoke to him more than any other. A thought that resonated with him somehow, even though he didn't want it to.

Maybe you can do better for the boy.

Maybe you can be exactly what he needs.

And maybe he can be exactly what you need.

He shook his head and pushed those dark and dangerous thoughts away, and Carlton knew there was only one thing for it now.

He needed to end this madness.

He needed to get on with things.

He needed to crush those dark thoughts before they took hold completely.

He reached for his knife.

Took a deep, shaky breath.

And he walked over to the farmhouse door.

He opened it.

Saw Billy sitting there, blindfolded in the darkness.

You don't have to do this. You can be better. You can—

"I have to do this," he said.

He closed the door behind him.

Tightened his grip on the knife.

And he walked over to Billy.

There was only one way out of this now.

The hunt was over.

He had to kill this boy and end this madness, once and for all.

CHAPTER TWENTY-SEVEN

Aoife walked across the old crop fields and couldn't shake the feeling someone was watching.

The moonlight was completely suffocated by cloud, now. There was a smell of manure in the air, a relic from the past. She kept on hearing things all around her. Sounded like footsteps. Sounded like voices.

She kept on telling herself it was all in her head. That she couldn't hear anything at all. That she was just imagining things.

She tried to keep her focus ahead.

Tried to keep her focus on the task at hand.

Finding Billy.

Finding that man who had kidnapped him.

And she was on his trail. She was close. She knew it.

She could see footprints in the ground before her. Clear prints in the mud. She couldn't see blood anymore. She could barely see anything anymore.

The dark outlines of the barns either side of her.

Of a farmhouse, just up ahead.

She heard shuffling over to her right. Froze. Dead.

There was somebody in there.

Someone watching her.

Billy?

She wasn't sure. Something didn't feel right.

She stood there. Waited for another sound. The only sound was her blood racing through her skull. Her heart thumping in her chest, harder and harder and harder.

She didn't hear anything else from inside the barn.

She turned around. Looked back at the footprints. They were leading right the way through the farmyard and towards the farmhouse.

She knew she had to be quiet. And she knew she had to be careful. This guy, the one who'd taken Billy, she couldn't mess around. The second she saw him, she had to be decisive. There could be no fucking around, and there could be no delay.

The moment she saw him, she had to act.

She didn't care about his backstory. She didn't care about his history.

She only cared about the fact that he'd taken Billy from her.

And she was going to make sure he paid for that.

She went to walk towards the farmhouse when she heard the noise again.

Scraping.

Footsteps.

In the barn right beside her.

She lifted her knife. Stood still. Totally still. Stared into the darkness.

There was someone in there.

There was someone in there, and they were watching her.

She couldn't just ignore it.

She had to investigate.

She walked towards it. Slowly.

Held her knife so tightly, her palm turning numb.

Her head spinning.

Her body weak, so weak, something she'd been able to forget

about for a moment because of how much adrenaline had taken over, seized control.

She crept over towards that dark void.

Knife raised.

Ready to act and ready to strike at a moment's notice.

Just hoping to God, she didn't collapse, or get ambushed, or the whole host of other things that could go tits up right now.

She reached the darkness when suddenly something jumped out.

She pulled back her knife.

Then she froze.

A cow.

A cow, standing there, staring right at her.

She let out a sigh. Shit. A working farm.

A working farm.

Which meant there were people here.

She wasn't alone here.

She patted the cow on its head. It moved away from her, shyly. She looked around. Looked at this farmyard. Was this where the guy was from? She wasn't sure. Couldn't be sure.

But it added up.

The blood on the road.

The trail of footprints.

It was a long shot, she knew.

But it was the only shot she had.

"Who's been looking after you, hmm?" she asked as she stroked the cow's head again. Its sandpaper tongue licked at her hands, so much rougher than anyone expected. "Who's been looking after you?"

She looked around the darkness of the farmyard, and she knew she couldn't delay any longer.

She went to walk when she felt a pain in her legs.

She froze. Stopped. Wobbled from side to side. Her head. A shooting pain in her head, right up her spine.

She wasn't out of the dark just yet.

She was still in danger.

She was still at risk.

"Come on," Aoife said, taking a few deep breaths. "You're going to be okay. You've got this. Everything's gonna be fine."

She walked a few more steps, following the footprint trail, when she tumbled forward again. Her balance was off, completely off. And it didn't feel like the breathing was helping her feel any better. If anything, she felt *worse*.

"Keep it together, Aoife. Keep it together."

She walked a few more steps, and she found her balance returning. She found herself feeling stronger. Feeling more confident. Feeling like she could make it.

But what if you make it to the farmhouse? What then? You're not strong enough. You're weak. You can barely stand. How the hell are you going to help Billy?

No. She couldn't think like that. She was strong. She always had been strong.

She wasn't letting Billy down.

"I'll find you," she said, putting one foot in front of the other, struggling to stay on her feet. "I'll... I'll find you, and I'll help you. I'll find you, and I'll save you. And then—and then we'll make it to safety. We'll find a new home. We'll..."

A sinking feeling in her stomach.

A twisting, churning pain in her chest.

A sense of inevitability taking over her.

She wasn't going to stay on her feet here.

She was going to fall.

She tried to keep her balance, but it was in vain.

She fell forward.

Tasted cold mud.

Stagnant water all in her nostrils.

She lay there a few seconds. Tried to push herself to her feet, but she was too weak.

"You have to get up," she said. "You have to."

But it didn't matter how hard she tried.

She was stuck here.

She was too weak to get up.

She lay there in the mud of this dark farmyard, and a sense of total defeat came over her.

She'd failed.

She'd failed Billy.

She was going to die here.

She went to push herself up, to try weakly again once more, when suddenly she heard something.

Footsteps.

Footsteps approaching her.

Someone was here.

CHAPTER TWENTY-EIGHT

Billy heard the door open and felt full of fear.

He was blindfolded, and it was dark. Or at least it was dark when he'd been blindfolded anyway. He didn't know so much anymore. It didn't matter anyway. He was tied at the wrists. And he was tied at the ankles. And he didn't have any way of escaping. Didn't have any way of getting out of... well, whoever this place was.

He was gagged. He couldn't say a word. He couldn't scream. He was trapped in here.

He thought back to earlier—or to whenever it was—and he felt sad. When he'd made a break for it. When he'd tried to get away. Tried to escape. And then Carlton had appeared out of nowhere, and he'd captured him. Stopped him. Taken him back.

Told him that was all a part of the fun.

That Billy was never really close to escaping at all.

That he was just doing this all for fun.

That's when he realised he wasn't going to escape this man.

He sat there in the dark and listened to the footsteps move across the cold, dusty room. He was shaking. No matter how much he tried to disappear someplace else in his mind or escape to somewhere nicer, like he used to be able to do with Ramiro and his men, this was different now.

He felt more fearful now. More afraid now.

Terrified.

He listened to those footsteps get closer and closer, and he didn't know what was coming next. He didn't have a clue. But he had an idea. That man. Carlton. He'd seen the look in his eyes. He'd seen how scary he looked. How monstrous he looked. And that was it. That was exactly it. He looked like a monster.

One of the monsters under his bed.

The kind he hid from.

The kind everyone tried to convince him wasn't real.

He looked like one of those monsters. Like there was something not human about him. Something scarier about him.

He heard those footsteps get closer and closer, and then they stopped.

He sat there. Not that he had a choice in the matter. Sat there and listened. Listened for more footsteps. Listened for breathing. Listened for any sign of life. Any sign that Carlton was in here with him.

But he didn't hear a thing.

And he wondered if this was all part of a game. If this was Carlton just trying to freak him out again. He wondered if he was doing the same thing he'd done before but differently. He definitely seemed to get something out of scaring people.

Scaring him.

He waited, listened for footsteps, listened for breathing.

And then, suddenly, he felt his head jolt forward a little, and he could see.

He couldn't see *well*. But he could see *enough*.

Part of him wished he couldn't see at all.

Carlton leaned over him. Stared down at him. He could only see the dark silhouette of his body and his face.

But he could see his eyes, too. Wide. Bright. Like they were glowing in the dark. Staring down at him. Bloodshot and angry red.

Snarl across his face.

He opened his mouth. Like he was going to say something to him. Looked like he had a lot to say.

And then his mouth closed. He looked away. Sighed.

"You're causing me a real old problem," Carlton said. "A bigger damned problem than I like to admit."

Billy didn't know what he meant by that. But as his eyes adjusted to the light—to the darkness—he could see a different expression to Carlton's face.

He looked like he wasn't sure. Like he was conflicted somehow.

He looked back at Billy, right into his eyes, and his face had changed again. He looked mad. Looked angry. His eyes darting around Billy's face, peering at him closely, trying to read his soul.

"What are we going to do with you, hmm?" Carlton asked. "What are we going to do with you?"

He stared at him a little while longer. It felt like forever.

And then he stuck the knife towards his face.

Tore his gag away.

Dragged it out of his mouth.

Billy coughed. Coughed so much he almost vomited. The gag tasted nasty, and it'd been stuffed right into his mouth.

"Now," Carlton said. "Now you have a chance to speak. Why don't you speak? You've got an opportunity. So go on. Speak up. Treat them like your last words, boy. 'Cause they might well be."

Billy felt tears stinging his eyes. He wanted to cry. He wanted to beg.

But he didn't.

He took a deep breath.

Gritted his teeth.

"I know you want me to be scared. I know—I know you want to see me afraid. But I won't... I won't give you that."

Carlton's head turned. His eyes narrowed. He looked genuinely surprised.

"I... I've been through bad things. Very bad things. Worse than this. I've—I've been through things where I've wanted to die. Where—where that's seemed better than what I was going through. And I've been... I've been far more scared than I am now. I'm not afraid of you. So do... do whatever you have to do. But I won't cry, and I won't be scared."

Carlton looked at him closely. Peered right into his eyes.

"Do it," Billy said. "Do—do whatever you have to do."

Carlton's eyes moved around his face, scanning him even more.

He stared at him. Silent for a long, long time.

And then, eventually, he let out a sigh.

And a long smile stretched across his face.

"Thank you for making the decision easier for me," he said.

He stood up.

Put the knife to Billy's face.

"But you know what?"

He pressed the knife against his nose.

Pushed harder, so Billy felt it hurting.

Tasted blood.

"I think I'm going to take your little thing about not being afraid of me as a challenge."

He pushed the knife harder to his nose.

His smile widened.

Fear rose in Billy's stomach.

He wanted to cry.

He wanted to scream.

But he couldn't.

He had to stay strong.

He had to—

Suddenly, the pain in his nose got hotter and harder.

He felt the knife slicing through his flesh.

And as a tear rolled down his cheek, Billy clenched his jaws together.

He wanted to cry out.

He wanted to scream.

He wanted to—

And then, out of nowhere, outside, he heard something.

A scream.

CHAPTER TWENTY-NINE

Aoife opened her eyes.

She didn't even realise she'd closed them. Last thing she remembered, she'd fallen down face first in the muddy farmyard. Certainly didn't feel like she was in a muddy farmyard anymore. Where the fuck was she?

She looked around. It was still dark. But there was a candle flickering somewhere over to her left. On a windowsill.

Outside, she saw nothing but darkness and heard the rain lashing down.

A sudden urgency filled her body. Billy. She was searching for Billy. Following his footprints in the mud. And then she'd fallen sick again. Collapsed to the ground. And then...

Fuck. She'd fucking passed out again, hadn't she? Honestly, it was getting beyond a joke at this stage. Becoming a frigging cliché.

Note to self: don't fucking pass out again. It's not a good look, and it's basically getting embarrassing at this point.

She looked around the room she was in. 'Cause she sure as shit wasn't outside anymore. It felt warm in here. It felt... nice. Comfortable. Was that a bed she was lying on? Fuck, it was the softest mattress she'd come across since she was at Sanctuary, probably.

She lay there. Squinted around in the darkness. Couldn't see a thing. Only that she was in some kind of bedroom, obviously. Kind of went without saying.

She went to sit up, fully expecting to be cuffed down by some lunatic psycho.

But she was free.

Her ankles were free.

Her wrists were free.

She was okay.

She went to climb off the side of the bed when suddenly a pain hit her.

A jarring pain. Harder than anything she'd ever felt. It was sort of in her right arm. Only... she wasn't sure. It felt distant, somehow. It felt like it was coming from a weird space beyond her arm. Impossible to describe.

But it was agony.

She wanted to look at her arm. Wanted to see. Maybe she'd hurt it in the fall.

But it was just too dark.

She collapsed back onto the bed because she felt dizzy.

That's when she heard footsteps.

Her chest tightened. She tensed up all over. Someone was coming. Someone was coming, and they were going to come in here and...

Shit.

What if it was the man?

What if it was the man who'd taken Billy?

She looked around the room, around the darkness, head spinning, feeling exhausted, and tried to find something she could use to defend or protect herself with.

But it was already too late.

The door creaked open.

A woman stood there. Holding a candlelit torch, which illuminated her face. She was old. Hunched over. Smirking away. She looked well-fed. Very well-fed. Alarmingly so. Kind of looked like one of those creepy old women you see in horror movies. That smile was more sinister than it was reassuring.

"Hello, dear. Lovely to see you awake. You must be thirsty."

She walked towards Aoife—crept across the bedroom floor, barely making a sound.

Aoife shook her aching head. "More... more confused."

"You're bound to be confused," the woman said. "You've been through an awful lot in an awfully short space of time. But don't you worry. You're in safe hands. We're looking after you."

Aoife felt the cup of water at her lips before she could ask any more questions and sipped away at it. She didn't get it. She didn't understand. Where was she? And what had happened to her?

"That's it," the woman said, moving the cup away, making Aoife cough a bit more. "Good to stay hydrated. You were in a bad way when we found you. Need to get you hydrated. And need to get you well-fed. You're skinny as they come. Lucky for you, we've lots of eggs here. Lots and lots and lots of milk. Fresh, from the cows."

The thought of eggs and milk made Aoife want to vomit right now.

"But don't you worry yourself about that. Not yet. You just focus on resting. We've got a little from you already. A sample. And lucky for you... you're going to be very well fed. You went down exceptionally well."

That smile.

Those big white teeth glowing in the orange of the candlelight.

And then a memory.

A flash of a memory in her mind.

Pain.

Agonising pain across her right arm.

Screaming.

"But don't you worry yourself about that now. In your time here, you'll be well looked after. You'll be very well fed. And you'll be... enjoyed. You'll be enjoyed."

She didn't like how the woman said those words. *You'll be enjoyed.*

She didn't like what they implied.

She didn't *know* what they implied.

But they worried her.

Crept her the fuck out.

"I'll leave your candle here," the woman said. "For some light. I'm sorry it's not much. But hopefully, it'll do."

Aoife watched her walk away. Creep across the room.

"Who... who are you?" Aoife asked.

The woman looked back at her. A big smile on her face. "I'm Joyce. I live at the farm here with my family. You'll meet them all soon, in due course. Rest, dear. Rest."

Aoife had so many questions. She wanted to get up. She wanted to find Billy.

"There... there was a boy," Aoife said.

Joyce stopped.

Looked around at her.

Her smile had dropped.

"What?"

"I was... I tracked a boy. To your farm. He's with someone. A man. A man kidnapped him. I think... I don't know where they went, but I think they're here. You need to get the boy away from the man. He's... he's dangerous. Please."

The woman stood there. Very still. Silent for a while.

Then that smile of hers returned.

"You're a godsend, you know? A godsend, my dear. You've no idea how much you've helped our case. But you'll be treated extra kindly for that. Now go on. Get yourself some rest."

"What do..."

But Aoife didn't get to ask Joyce anything else because the door closed behind her and left her in this candlelit room, alone.

She lay there a few seconds. Trying to get her head around all this weirdness. What the fuck was Joyce talking about, helping her out? What did any of it mean?

She went to look at the bedside table at her side when something caught her eye.

The source of that pain.

The source of that agony on her arm.

There was something wrong.

Something very wrong.

She lay there and stared at her right arm, and she realised, with growing dread, just how much shit she was in.

Her right arm ended at the elbow.

It was bandaged there. A little bloody. But bandaged.

And nothing beyond her elbow.

"What... How..."

She stared at her arm. No. Fuck. This couldn't be real. This couldn't be true. This had to be a nightmare. This had to be a fucking nightmare.

You'll be very well fed. And you'll be enjoyed...

"No," Aoife said. "No!"

And as much as Aoife wanted to keep her shit together, she let out a scream.

CHAPTER THIRTY

Carlton heard the scream.

He stopped. Stopped with the knife right to Billy's nose. He'd just started digging the fucking sharp edge of it in, too. Just started cutting that little fucker's skin and flesh away.

And he wasn't getting the same joy from it. That was the problem. He wasn't getting the joy he expected from it, the joy he *wanted* from it. The joy he'd been anticipating for so, so long.

Something was wrong.

He knew he needed to up the stakes. He knew he needed to make things more interesting. More exciting. He didn't know *how* exactly to do it. But he could get creative. He was lucky in that regard, had a very creative mind.

But that scream. The scream cutting through his focus, through his concentration, through his fantasy and his dreaming.

He stopped. Stopped as the little kid's blood trickled down his fingers. As he gasped and whimpered and tried not to cry.

Looked back. Back towards the door to this little outhouse in the farm, he'd found. He was sure he was alone here. Pretty sure, anyway.

But it definitely sounded like someone was close.

And that wasn't good.

Or maybe it was...

The scream. Maybe it was someone he could add to the fun here. Maybe it was someone he could capture and bring down here and try to get a little excitement out of.

Because right now, no matter how much he told himself this was what he needed to do... he heard that rival voice in his head. Louder than ever before.

Maybe you're changing.

Maybe this boy is different.

Maybe you don't want to kill him.

Maybe you like him because you see yourself in him...

"No!" Carlton said.

And he felt stupid about it right away. He felt weak. Because he knew the boy was looking at him. He knew he'd see him losing his shit like this. And he'd think he was crazy. He'd think he was mad.

And maybe he was crazy. Maybe he was mad. But this wasn't the kind of crazy and mad he wanted to put across.

He looked at Billy. Looked into his eyes. Looked at the blood oozing out of that slice on his left nostril. He'd take that little piggy nose off his face in a flash.

As soon as he investigated that scream.

"You wait here, kiddo. Not that you're going anywhere."

He smirked at him.

And then he turned around.

Walked over to the door.

Popped his head outside.

He looked to the right. Then to the left.

Nothing.

Nothing but darkness.

Nothing but rain falling.

Nothing but the occasional flash of lightning, another storm, right in the distance.

He stepped back into the outhouse when he heard the scream again.

He stopped. Froze. A woman. She sounded weak. She sounded vulnerable.

And he felt jealous.

He wanted to be the one causing that trauma.

He wanted to be the one causing that pain.

He looked back. Looked at Billy. Sitting there. Tied up. Not moving a muscle. Just staring at him with those wide eyes.

"I won't be long," Carlton said. "And you bet we'll pick up where we left off. Right where we left off."

He winked at him. Tried to look calm and confident. But truth be told, he was pretty spooked.

Felt creeped out. Felt rattled.

He turned around and walked outside, into the rain, towards the screams. The smell of cow shit strong in the air. So strong he could taste it. He could hear movement to his left. Looked around and saw a cow poking its head out.

He walked over to it.

Put a hand on its head.

"Hey, buddy. You seen anything weird around here?"

The cow licked at his arm with that rough tongue.

He thought about grabbing it.

Thought about yanking it right out.

Thought about slicing that knife right through it.

He put his knife to its head.

Pushed down, just a little.

Then he sighed and moved his knife away.

"Congrats. Today's your lucky day."

He walked away. Hands in his pockets. Towards that farmhouse. The wind was getting stronger, the rain getting heavier. Storm was really picking up.

He walked across the yard, and suddenly he saw someone standing right ahead.

He froze. Someone standing right there. Looked like a bloke. A biggish bloke at that.

"Well, hello," he said, to himself more than anyone. "What do we have here?"

He tightened his grip around his knife. Licked his dry lips. Hell, maybe this was what he needed. Getting a bit spooked before having some fun.

Maybe it'd make everything that happened next all the more exciting.

He walked towards that figure when suddenly he caught something in the periphery of his vision, and he knew he'd fucked up.

A crack.

A crack right across his head.

Falling to the ground.

Hitting the mud.

He turned around. Tried to shift onto his back.

And when he looked up, he saw two of them.

A man and a woman.

Both grinning away.

Both holding candles.

"Come on," the bloke on the right said. "Let's get you inside. And let's get that boy of yours while we're at it."

He tried to fight back, tried to shake free, tried to resist.

But the next thing he knew, he felt a cloth cover his face, his mouth, his nostrils, and as much as he tried to fight, as much as he tried not to inhale, the ghastly fumes filled his lungs, made him dizzy, made him sleepy, made him...

Nothing but darkness.

CHAPTER THIRTY-ONE

Billy looked out of the open door into the darkness, and he really wanted to get away.

His nose was sore. Really sore. He was shaking. Trying his best not to look scared in front of Carlton. But it was hard. Because he *was* scared. He didn't want to hurt again. And he didn't want to die.

He'd seen the look in Carlton's eyes. He'd seen the way he'd smiled as he pushed that blade into the flesh on his nose. And the scary thing was that he knew it was just the start. Carlton wanted him to hurt—bad. He didn't know why, but he was mean, cruel, and wanted to cause him pain.

But he'd heard that scream. And he'd gone out of the door.

And then Billy heard some shouting and fighting, and he knew something had happened.

He sat there. His wrists were tied. His ankles were tied. He tried to move, but he was stuck. He wondered if maybe this was like before when Carlton let him run and then caught him. Maybe this was all a game. Maybe he was trying to get him to hope again. Trying to make him think he could get out, trying to make him think he could get away. Only to capture him again.

He didn't know why Carlton was doing this. He seemed a mean, nasty man. And he knew there were a lot of mean, nasty men in this world.

He just hoped Aoife was okay.

He thought about her lying under that wreckage, totally still. He didn't know if she was alive or dead. But he wanted to go back for her. He wanted her to be okay.

But there was nothing he could do.

Not stuck here.

He tried to shuffle forward, but he couldn't move. He was on a chair, and he was stuck. The only thing he could try was toppling the chair, making it fall over. But then he'd be stuck.

He looked around the room he was in. Some kind of cold dark room, a garage, or something like that.

And as he squinted into the darkness, he tried to find something he could use to get him out. Something sharp. Anything at all.

But he didn't see anything.

He didn't see...

In the corner of his eyes, out of nowhere, like he'd wished it up himself, he saw it.

Hanging on the wall.

A pair of those big scissor things. He didn't know what they were called, but he'd seen Mum using them in the garden to cut plants and do other boring things.

They looked dirty and rusty, but it was something. They were on the other side of this building.

But if he could get to them, at least he could try.

"Check out the outhouse," he heard someone say. "Swear I heard something over there."

Billy froze. Someone was coming for him. And it didn't sound like Carlton.

And even though he was more scared of Carlton than

anyone... he still didn't want to take his chances on whoever was coming.

He just wanted to get out of here and get away.

He tried to shake his chair, but it just shuffled a little bit. Tried to wobble to the wall. He didn't know if he could make it. And he didn't know how he would grab the big sharp scissor things when he got to them.

But he was going to try.

He had to try.

He shuffled to the right again. Felt the chair legs wobbling like when Harriet Davidson leaned back on it in school and fell back and cracked her head against the table behind her. Split open her head and needed stitches. Stopped anyone doing it again. So much blood. Such loud screams.

He felt himself hovering in the air as the stool wobbled on its side. He heard the footsteps getting closer. Someone whistling. Sounded like a man.

He needed to be quick.

Very quick.

He wobbled that chair even further, harder than before.

And this time, he toppled over. Landed on his side.

A bigger bang than he was expecting.

"Shit," a voice said. "Definitely someone in there."

He lay there on his side. Face stinging. So sore and so tired and so scared.

He had to figure out what to do now.

He had to try something.

He tried dragging himself across the floor like a worm, but he was stuck.

He tried standing up, but his knees were weak, his ankles were tied, and he was in an even worse position now than before.

He tried to get around onto his knees, to sit up, but it was no use.

He wasn't going to make it to the big scissor things.

He was stuck.

He went to push himself one final time when suddenly he heard a whistle at the door.

He looked around.

A man was standing there.

He couldn't see him very well. But in the moonlight, he looked tall. And he looked pale.

And he was smiling.

Even scarier looking than Carlton.

"Well, well," the man said. "You okay there, little one?"

Billy stayed still. Very still. Didn't say a word.

The man walked into the outhouse. Walked towards Billy. Slowly. Raised his hands. "You don't have to worry, little fella. We're here to help you. That bad man tie you up in here? Real mean of him, hmm?"

And Billy didn't know what to say to him. The man seemed friendly. He was smiling.

But Billy had a bad feeling about him.

He didn't trust him.

"You just stay still, buddy. You just stay very still. And I'll get you out of that mess. I'll get you out..."

Billy wasn't sure if he kept talking.

Because he saw something, then.

Something that made his stomach drop.

A hand.

A hand dangling around his neck.

Grey and pale and smelly.

He looked at it. And he saw the bald man look down at it, then back up at Billy. A look in his eyes like he knew. He knew Billy knew. And that made him feel scared. He wished he hadn't noticed him looking.

"Don't worry about my special necklace," the man said. "Just do as I say, and you won't have to worry about a thing."

Billy stayed still.

Even though he didn't want to.

There was nothing else he could do.

The man grabbed his arms. He put his knife against the ties around his wrists and ankles. Cut against them.

"That's it," he said. "Almost done. You just stay still. You just..."

The second Billy was free, he didn't stop to think.

He banged his head against the man's face.

And then he got up, and he ran.

Grabbed the handle of those big scissor things on the wall—

A hand around his ankle.

He fell to the floor. Slammed against it.

The big scissors in his hand.

"Little shit," the man said. "You little shit. How dare you. I was trying to help you. I was trying to make things easier on you. Not anymore, you little brat. Not anymore."

He swung Billy around, so he was looking right into his eyes.

Billy held the big scissor things in front of him.

The man's eyes widened. "What..."

Billy didn't stop to think.

He pushed those big scissors up into his chest, right between the ribs, right where he thought the man's heart was.

He buried them in there. Buried them deep. Kept on pushing. Kept on going.

Felt hot blood trickling down from him.

Tasted it in the air like pennies.

The man coughed. Spluttered. More blood oozed out of him as Billy held on to those big scissors. As his shaking hands pushed them even harder into the man's chest.

He wobbled over to the side. Hit the floor.

The big scissors sticking out of his chest.

Billy dragged himself back. He stood up, covered in blood. Shaking.

He looked down at that man. Watched him trying to pull the

scissors out of his chest but not being able to. Too shaky. Too weak.

"I'm sorry," Billy said. "I..."

He heard more voices outside. And he knew he couldn't stay here. He knew he had to move.

He walked over to the door. Looked out into the night. It was dark again. Rainy again. Looked stormy.

He looked around over towards a farmhouse. Fields around it. Two people there, walking along, dragging Carlton along with them, over to that house, over towards where he'd heard the scream.

He watched him get dragged away, and he got a weird feeling.

Even though he'd hurt him. Even though he'd put him through pain.

He felt weirdly sorry for Carlton.

He didn't think he was bad out of choice.

He felt like he was just bad to the core.

And that made him different...

He took a deep breath of the cold night air. Looked back around at the man he'd stabbed. He'd gone quiet now. Twitching. But quiet.

And then he turned back around and stepped out into the darkness.

He was going to find Aoife.

And he was going to get to Rhyl.

Together, they were going to make it.

CHAPTER THIRTY-TWO

Aoife lay back in the bed and still couldn't wrap her head around the nightmare she was facing.

She didn't want to look at her arm. Or rather, where her forearm once was. She didn't want to see it. Because seeing it was just a reminder. A reminder of what'd happened. A reminder of what she'd lost.

A reminder of just how weak she was now.

She felt sick. She'd screamed for God knows how long, only to pass out and wake up and scream again, then pass out again. Her body was exhausted. She didn't know if she'd ever get out of this bed again. She didn't know if she'd ever stand again. If she'd ever walk again.

She just felt completely and utterly broken.

She looked around in the darkness. Colours filled her vision. Big blobs of light flashed in the corners of her eyes. Breathing was an effort. Moving was an effort. *Everything* was an effort.

She just couldn't stop thinking about what'd happened to her.

About what that creepy old woman, Joyce, said.

You're a godsend. And you'll be treated extra kindly for that.

She didn't know what she meant. She didn't know why she'd done this to her. Why she'd mutilated her in this way. What she wanted with her.

But she feared she was stuck here.

She feared there was no getting out.

And then she thought of Billy, and she felt even more fucking scared.

She'd tracked Billy here. Well. She'd tracked the man who'd taken him, anyway. Or at least she thought she had. What if she'd been on the wrong trail all along? What if it wasn't Billy and that man she'd been following all this time?

And if it was...

What had happened to Billy?

Was that man one of these people?

She had no idea. Thinking itself was exhausting.

All she knew was that she was stuck. Stuck here on this bed. Missing half a fucking arm. Not chained up or anything. Not pinned down.

But she didn't have to be. They had her right where they wanted her, and they knew it.

She felt a tear roll down her face. That splitting pain in her right arm. It was impossible to explain. She'd heard about phantom limb pains before, in amputees and people who'd lost legs in wars, that kind of thing. But she'd always thought it must be some kind of psychological trick. She didn't believe it was actually a thing.

But lying here right now, feeling that burning pain right through where her right forearm used to be... feeling the hot pins and needles stabbing into every inch of that blank space... feeling that throbbing toothache-style agony hang there, so dull... and not being able to do a thing about it.

Yeah. Aoife felt pretty damned guilty for ever dismissing anyone claiming to have phantom limb pain in the past.

She turned onto her back again and stared up into the dark.

She wanted to do something. Wanted to be proactive. Wanted to move.

But at the same time... what *could* she do? She didn't have any energy. She didn't have any strength. She knew there was only one real outcome ahead for her. Losing an arm couldn't exactly help with that. Even though it seemed like they'd stitched it up surprisingly well. Even though it didn't seem to be bleeding that badly.

She knew she was on borrowed time. Already *was* on borrowed time. Her body had been through shit no body should have to go through. Shit no body was designed to go through.

And she was still here. Clinging on. Barely.

She closed her burning eyes and thought of Billy. Wherever she was, she hoped—prayed—he was okay. Even if, deep down, she feared the worst. She couldn't help fearing the worst.

What else was she supposed to think? That man she'd seen. Billy was afraid of him. He seemed ruthless. Dangerous.

Aoife just hoped Billy had enough about him to escape him. To get away from him.

He'd survived this far. Been through a shitload, sure. More than anyone should have to go through.

But he'd survived. That was the key thing. He'd made it this far.

He just had to make it a little further.

But then she opened her eyes.

Out of nowhere, a jolt of energy. A bolt of strength.

So she was just going to lie here?

She was just going to lie in this bed and give up?

No. Was she fuck.

That wasn't who she was.

She didn't care whether it was the end for her. She didn't care what happened next. If she stayed here, her fate was certain anyway.

She might as well try something.

She held her breath and turned herself onto her left side.

Agony. Pure agony from head to toe. Splitting. Burning. Tearing.

She let out a little cry. Her throat was sore, so raw. Nothing more than a gasp came out of her dry, chapped lips.

The pain was intense. And it didn't seem to be getting any better. If anything, it was getting worse.

But you're strong, Aoife. You're strong. And you don't quit. You don't give up. You never give up.

She thought of Max. Thought of what he'd say to her. Thought of how much he'd encourage her.

Encourage her to step up.

To keep fighting.

No matter what.

She took as deep a breath as she could, right into her sore lungs.

And then she tightened a fist.

"I can get out of this. I can do this."

She went to lift herself up from the bed when she heard a door open.

Light filled the dark room.

That woman, Joyce, standing there with that candle in hand.

Two other people by her side. Men. Both pale. Both grey-faced. Both so, so tall.

And there was somebody between them.

Another man.

"We've got some company for you, dear," Joyce said.

She stepped aside. And as much as Aoife's vision was blurry, as much as it was a struggle to make anything out... she saw the man they were dragging in, and everything else froze.

He was badly beaten. Bruised. Bleeding.

But it was him.

"You two settle down. You've got a long day ahead of you tomorrow."

But Aoife couldn't think about a thing.
It was the man who'd taken Billy.
He was here.

But Aoife couldn't think about a thing.
It was the man who'd taken Billy.
He was here.

CHAPTER THIRTY-THREE

Billy didn't stop running until it was light.

He fell over and hit the muddy ground. Tasted the dirt and some blood, too, like pennies. He used to like the taste of pennies. Grandma used to always tell him off for sucking them. Told him they were dirty. But he didn't care. Not until he choked on one.

He'd never forget the dread he'd felt when that happened. Coughing, spluttering, trying to breathe but not being able to stop himself.

But the one thing that made him feel calmer was Grandma. The way she held him. The way she slapped his back. *Ssh,* she said. *It'll be okay. Just keep coughing. Just let it happen.*

As Billy lay there in the dirt, face down, heart beating fast, finding it hard to breathe, he wished Grandma was here to make him feel better. He wished she was here to tell him everything would be okay. That he just had to stay calm.

He wished a lot of people were here. Aoife too.

He looked up. Saw tall grass in front of him. He'd been running across fields for what felt like forever. He kept thinking he heard things. Movement. People chasing him. And a part of him couldn't help worrying that maybe this was all a game, too. That Carlton was playing with him, just like yesterday. That he was making it look like he could get away, giving him hope, only to take it from him right when he thought he was away.

He looked back. Back through the tall grass. He thought he saw movement. He thought he heard voices, and he thought he heard footsteps.

But then he took a breath.

There was nobody following him.

Someone had taken Carlton.

He was going to be okay.

He pushed himself back to his feet. He felt wobbly, and he felt weak. He'd been running for so long. He didn't know how long, but it had to be a long time because it wasn't light when he started running.

He needed to find some shelter. He needed to get some rest.

But he didn't want to give up on Aoife.

He'd been searching for the train tracks for a long time. For the railway line. He knew that if he could find that, he could get to Aoife.

He didn't know what sort of state Aoife was in. He didn't even know if she was still alive. She didn't seem very alive when he'd walked away from her. If she was still under that wreckage after last night... he dreaded to think what state she'd be in.

But he didn't want to give up on her. He didn't want to just leave her there.

He'd made her a promise. And he was going to keep it.

Especially after everything she'd done for him.

He thought about Rhyl. About North Wales, where she said the good place was. The community. And he knew she'd want him to go there. He knew she'd want him to keep on going. He knew she wouldn't want him going back for her, especially when it looked like she was already in big, big trouble.

"But I'm not giving up on you," he said. "You risked everything for me. I'm not leaving you behind."

He went to walk when he heard something up ahead.

Footsteps.

Voices.

He stopped. Froze. Dropped down in the tall grass, hiding. He didn't know who it was. He didn't need to know who it was.

Just that he had to hide from them.

Just that they couldn't see him.

Because he didn't want to run into anyone else out here.

He knew he sounded silly. He'd been telling Aoife she had to trust people more. That it was the only way they'd ever find a new home.

But now he was on his own... he got it. He understood.

He was scared of other people.

He wanted to trust them, but he was scared of them.

The only thing he wasn't scared of was the community Aoife had told him about.

He trusted her. And he trusted them.

He kept low as footsteps got closer. Definitely wasn't imagining things this time. There was someone here, and they were getting closer. He could hear talking. Couldn't hear what they were saying but sounded like men.

And he'd had enough bad experiences with men to panic right now. To feel sick about things right now.

He stayed very still. Shaking in the grass. Hoped they weren't walking right towards him. Hoped they wouldn't find him. Hoped everything was going to be okay.

He heard their footsteps so, so close.

And then they stopped.

Out of nowhere, they stopped.

He lay there. Kept still. Didn't move. They'd stopped. He couldn't hear them. Or maybe they'd walked another way. He wasn't sure.

He just knew he had to keep quiet.

And then he had to move.

He waited there a little longer, and then he heard something that made him feel relieved.

Those footsteps. They were walking away from him.

He stood up. Walked the other way, slowly. He had to back away. He had to run. He had to get away from them.

He started to run when suddenly he felt something block his way.

He froze.

He didn't want to look around at what it was.

Didn't want to see.

But he had no choice.

He turned around and saw a man standing there.

Looking down at him.

Smile on his face.

Rifle in hand.

"Going somewhere, kid?" he asked.

CHAPTER THIRTY-FOUR

Aoife saw the man sitting in the corner of the room, back up against the wall, and she didn't even know where to start.

It was him. The man who'd kidnapped Billy. The man who'd chased Billy through the train and scared Billy earlier on. Who'd pushed that body down the hill, right towards them. Terrorising them for some bizarre reason.

He was here.

He looked in a bad way. She couldn't see very well in the dark, and her vision was properly blurred, too. But she could see his eyes were swollen. She could see cuts over his face. Bruises every-where. Looked like they'd really put him through shit.

But seeing him here in this room, seeing him in the state he was in, at least she knew he wasn't with these people. The ones who had captured her and him.

And there was something else, too.

Billy.

Where the hell was Billy?

"You'd better get talking," Aoife said. She barely had any strength. But just seeing this man had made her feel stronger, somehow. Because he was the one who'd kidnapped Billy. She'd tracked him here. She was right—he *had* gone this way.

And now she wanted some answers.

The man tilted his head. Squinted across the room at her. He wasn't handcuffed or anything. Looked like the people here—wherever here was—had a lot of confidence that their prisoners weren't going to escape.

He stared at her closely. Smiled. Like he recognised her. "There's something different about you."

"Don't bullshit me about anything right now. I don't... I don't have the strength left for bullshit—"

"Your arm. Damn. They did that? The people here did that?"

"And I'll do far, far worse to you if you don't start talking."

The man coughed. Sounded like his throat was thick with phlegm and blood. "What do you want to know?"

There was a real creepy air about the guy. He spoke with this strange voice that sent shivers up Aoife's spine. "You know exactly what I want to know. Billy. Where the hell is he? And what have you done with him?"

The man's smile widened. She saw blood between his bright white teeth. Like he was enjoying this. "The boy. Billy. Ah. I think I remember who you're talking about."

Aoife went to launch herself forward but immediately fell back. She was too weak to do anything at all.

The man laughed a little. His laugh turned into a cough. Sounded raw. Like he was in bad pain too. "Look at you. Lying there, missing an arm, thinking you're all strong. Thinking you're all threatening. And thinking there's anything you can do to get what you want from me."

He stood up, then. Limped over to the side of the bed. Looked down at her. Right at her arm, with wide-eyed fascination.

"See, that's the thing about me," he said.

Moving his hand down her arm.

Right towards the bandaged wound.

He stopped his hand, just before it.

That smile still stretched across his face.

"Life's all just a game. And I'm the only one who knows how to play."

He squeezed the wound, then. Squeezed it hard.

Aoife lurched back. Screamed. Agony. Even worse than anything she'd felt already. Burning and stinging like she'd never felt before, like a thousand bees were attacking her, again and again, and again.

And then he let go and stepped back. Dropped her arm, which hurt even more as it hit the bed.

She reached for it, whimpering, crying, feeling so, so in pain, so, so weak. Like she was going to pass out again.

"Your boy," the man said. "He's put us in an interesting predicament, let's say."

Aoife couldn't speak. She didn't know what this guy was talking about.

He walked around to the foot of the bed. Wiped the blood from Aoife's arm onto his coat. "You worry about him. And I understand that. It sounds like you were close. It certainly *looked* like you were close. Maybe not mother and child close... but I could sense something there. Definitely something very, very sweet about it."

"Just tell me... tell me what you did with him."

He smirked again. Laughed. "What would the fun in that be?"

She lay back. Lay against the pillow. She felt so hopeless. So helpless. Because she wanted to fight this guy. She wanted to kick the shit out of him for withholding this information from her. She at least wanted to let him know how she felt.

But she didn't have the strength, and she didn't have the energy, and there was nothing she could do about it.

She didn't want to give up.

But what could she do?

"Okay," he said. "Okay. I'm looking at the situation we're in, and I'm thinking... Look. I spared him, okay?"

Aoife frowned. A glimmer of hope through the pain. "Wh —what?"

"I spared him. I could have killed him. Believe me; I wanted to. But... well. In the end, fate was on the boy's side. And now here we are."

Aoife lay there. Shaking. He was alive? Billy was alive?

"Then where—where is he?"

"That, I don't know. I can't be sure. But I know where he was when these amateurs captured me. So if we can get out there, then maybe, just maybe, we might have a chance."

"We?" Aoife said.

The man's smile widened. "How rude of me not to introduce myself. My name's Carlton. People used to call me Carl. But let's just say I fancied a slight change."

Aoife shook her head. She didn't know what to say to this man. He was insane. Clearly insane.

But he was talking about getting out of here.

And he hadn't killed Billy.

Unless he was lying...

But then, why would he?

He walked back over to the side of her bed. Looked down at her and smiled.

"The way I see it... right now, we're stuck in here. Right now, neither of us is in the best shape. But our best chance of getting out of here?"

"Enlighten me."

"Together," he said.

Aoife shook her head. There were shades of her escape with Grace about this. Grace wanted revenge so badly that she'd come back to help her.

"Why keep me alive?"

"Because I'm an honest man who enjoys a good hunt. And the

way I see it... these amateurs here are standing in the way of a fair hunt. We get away from them. We escape. We work together. And then... well. The hunt for Billy can resume."

"You're fucking insane."

"Or maybe I'm completely sane. And you are the insane ones. Following your rules, even though the world as you know it is over. Fooling yourself with beliefs about morality and ethics when all those ideas were mere constructs of the world before. And maybe that's why I'm still here. Maybe that's why I'm happier than the rest of you. Because you're all so bloody dreary. All so darned miserable. Have you ever stopped to think about that?"

Aoife didn't know what to say. She just shook her head.

Because this guy. He sounded mad. He sounded crazy.

But he sounded genuine, too.

"So what do you say?" he asked. "Shall we get out of here? Because believe me. It's the only chance we're going to get."

Aoife didn't want to work with this guy. She didn't want to agree with anything he was proposing.

But in the end, what choice did she have?

She was on her deathbed. And whatever plan he proposed was surely better than the alternative.

"What the fuck," Aoife said. "I'm in."

Carlton smiled. He held out a hand towards her severed arm. And then he pulled it away. "Oh. I do apologise. Excuse my manners."

"The second we get out of here," Aoife said. "You're dead."

Carlton chuckled. Patted her right on her head. "That's the fighting spirit I like to see. Now. Should we get to work?"

Aoife had no idea what she was signing up to or what she was agreeing to.

But she found herself holding her breath and nodding.

"I can't believe I'm saying this. But let's get the hell out of this place."

CHAPTER THIRTY-FIVE

"Going somewhere, kid?"

Billy looked up at the man standing over him, and he felt scared.

The man was holding a gun. Pointing it right at him. He was dressed all in black. He had this big beard. And even though Ramiro's people were gone, Billy thought he looked like he could be from that group. He didn't look much different to them at all.

Especially the way he smiled at him.

Like Billy was nothing.

He lay in the tall grass. Felt the damp mud soaking through his clothes. He could hear other voices, too. Two more people, maybe. They'd found him. Whoever they were, they'd found him.

And they didn't seem like the kind of people Billy wanted to run into at all.

"A kid like you all alone out here. How's that happen, hmm?"

Billy swallowed a lump in his throat. He knew he wasn't going to get out of this without speaking. "I just... I got away. From somewhere."

"Oh, you got away from somewhere, did you? And where's that somewhere?"

Billy closed his burning eyes. He wanted to disappear. He wanted all this hell to be over. He wanted to be with Aoife, and he wanted to get to Rhyl and...

He needed to stop moping.

He needed to stop being weak.

He needed to be strong.

"It doesn't matter where I got away from," Billy said. "But I'm going somewhere. And it's—it's none of your business where."

He started to climb back to his feet. Shaky. He felt even weaker than before, in a way that he always did when he did something daring. Something scary.

The man pushed him down the second Billy got back to his feet.

Laughed at him.

"I appreciate the sentiment, kid. But the thing is... where I'm from, we lost a lot of property. A hell of a lot. And you know what the hottest property we had was?"

Billy lay there. Looking up into that man's eyes.

"Kids," he said.

The man reached down, then. Grabbed him. Lifted his sleeve.

"The mark of Ramiro," the man said. "Damn it. I almost feel for you. So far away from home. You coulda just kept on running the other way and you'd probably've made it away. We weren't going much further. But, hey. Rules are rules, huh?"

Billy tried to pull his arm away from the man's grip. The mark of Ramiro? He looked at that cross on his wrist. The one the man did with the knife a long time ago. Was that what it was? A mark to show he was one of Ramiro's?

He wanted to be strong. He wanted to fight.

But all he could say?

"Please."

The man chuckled. "Now ain't the time for begging. It's like I said. Rules are rules. I'd love to let you go wandering off into the wilds. Really, I would. But you ain't meant to be out here, kid.

You're property. Our property. But you don't have to worry. We'll look after you a whole lot better than Ramiro did."

"Jarrod," Billy said. "You... you're with Jarrod?"

The man loosened his grip just a little. Smirked. "Yeah. You are sharp, hmm? Tell me, lad. What do you know about Jarrod?"

Billy didn't know much about him. Only that Ramiro always sounded scared of him. That he'd been in some kind of fight with him. And that Jarrod's people had taken over Ramiro's camp in the end.

"I guess it don't really matter what you do or don't know, huh," he said. "Come on. Got a long walk ahead of us. We'll give you that much, tough man. Let you walk yourself. Don't want us carryin' you, eh? We'll spare you that embarrassment."

Billy felt that man's hand around his arm, tight. But a little looser than before.

He saw the tall grass.

He saw a chance to run.

One chance to try and run.

He went to move when the man just scooped him up and pulled him over his shoulder like he was nothing.

"Okay. You're a runner. Never mind, eh? Slows us down a bit. But at least you ain't gonna try nothin' no more."

Billy punched the man's back. He wasn't giving up. He was fighting. "Let me go!"

The man walked. Chuckled a bit. "I ain't doing no such thing."

Billy sunk his teeth into the man's back.

Bit down. Hard.

So hard he tasted blood.

"Shit," the man said.

He punched Billy. Punched him back down to the muddy ground.

Looked down at him, then pushed that rifle to his head.

"Listen, kid. I've had enough shit these last few days. The last thing I need is a little brat like you causing me problems. So you'd better do as I say. You'd better fucking behave. 'Cause if you don't behave, you believe me, I don't give a shit if I put a bullet through your head. What's one more dead kid lost on the road anyway, huh?"

"Then shoot me," Billy said, the taste of the man's blood strong in his mouth. "Shoot me 'cause—'cause I'll never stop fighting."

The man tilted his head. Sighed. "I'm giving you a chance here. A chance to live. You be careful what you say next—"

"He hurt me," Billy shouted. "He... he hurt so many of us. And it never stopped. I thought that was life. I thought that was what I had to look forward to. Ramiro and his people doing those things to me and the others again and again and again. And I... I got away. I got away, and I just want a chance. I want to live again. And if I can't... I don't want to live anymore. So let me go. Let me go, or I'll... I'll just keep fighting. I'll bite you again. I'll do everything I can. But I won't come with you."

The man stood there. Rifle pointed at Billy.

Shook his head.

"Well," he said. "That's quite the speech you put up there, little one. But it doesn't work that way."

He reached down to grab Billy again when out of nowhere, he heard something.

A gargle.

Choking.

And then he felt something.

Something warm.

Blood.

He looked up at the man as he reached towards him, as he went to lift him up. And he noticed something.

He was bleeding.

Holding his neck and bleeding.

The man staggered forward.

Fell down, right beside Billy.

Billy stared at him. Heart racing.

What'd happened to him?

There was a bloody hole in his neck.

Someone had done this to him.

Someone had...

It was right then that Billy heard something.

A growl.

An animal.

A nasty wolf was going to get him.

A monster.

The monsters were finally here, and they...

But then Billy saw it.

Right in front of him, right in the middle of that tall grass.

A dog.

Looked like a scary dog. Black and brown. With a weird little half-tail. Bloodshot red eyes and lots of drool down its chin.

It stared at him. Growling.

And he stared back at it.

He needed to run.

He needed to get away.

He went to take a step back when he saw someone appear beside the dog.

A woman.

Tall.

Thin.

Blonde.

Bright blue eyes.

And a smile.

"Well, Rex," she said. "What do we have here?"

CHAPTER THIRTY-SIX

"So, do you actually have a plan for getting out of here? Or are you just saying all that crap to make yourself feel better?"

The man, Carlton, didn't say anything. He didn't seem to be listening. Just kept on pacing around this dark room. Looking at the windows. Trying to open them. Scanning the floor and trying to find any loose floorboards. Trying the door handle, again and again, but the result was always the same.

There was no way out of here.

She watched him follow this routine again and again. She felt fucked, naturally. Her head was aching now, stronger than any headache she'd had in her entire life. She'd never had a migraine. Always pissed her off when people banged on about how bad they were. They were just glorified headaches, right? And was a headache really that bad?

But lying here, she sympathised with those whining bastards, now.

'Cause she felt like shit. Felt like something heavy was hanging in her skull. Hurt her eyes and ears just moving.

She wasn't getting better, that was for sure.

"Are you literally just pacing around the room?" Aoife said. "Is that your plan?"

"I'm thinking," Carlton said.

"You're thinking? This is what thinking looks like for you?"

He ignored her.

"Can you try thinking a little quieter?"

"Respectfully," Carlton said, turning around to face her. He had a mean, pissed-off look to his face now. Definitely didn't look like he was revelling in the thrill of the "hunt" or the "game" or whatever he'd called it before. "Respectfully... I've given you an opportunity here. An opportunity to help me escape this place. Because these people rudely interrupted what we had going on. I could kill you right now. I could strangle you, and I'd get a whole lot of a buzz from it. But I'd get even more of a buzz from playing the long game. But if me strangling you right now is the route you want to go down... please, just tell me."

Aoife shook her head. "You're actually fucking insane."

Carlton rolled his eyes. "Yeah, yeah. We've had that debate already. Hold on."

He had hold of a big painting on the right side of the room. It had waves on it and a load of other arty farty shit that Aoife wasn't interested in and didn't even want to understand.

"Is now really the time to be doing an art critique?" Aoife asked.

Carlton shook his head. "It's not the art I'm interested in. Beautiful as it is."

He put the painting down on the floor, and he knocked the wall.

His eyes lit back as he looked around at Aoife. "You hear that?"

"I hear you knocking on a wall."

"No. Listen closer."

He knocked on the wall. Then knocked to the side of the painting.

"I'm not sure I understand," Aoife said.

"It's hollow here. They must've put this wall in. Or this section of it anyway."

"Which means?"

"Which means there's a chance we can escape through it. Or at least use it to our advantage."

Aoife laughed. It hurt to laugh, but she couldn't help it.

"Something funny?" Carlton asked.

"So, what, you suggest we ram the wall down? We just go and knock it down while they're sitting in there doing whatever they're doing? And then what? End up in the room next door? Really? Listen to yourself."

Carlton's eyes narrowed. He didn't look like the kind of guy who took nicely to his ideas being criticised. Fucker.

"Do you have any better ideas?" he asked.

"I don't know," Aoife said. "Right now, I'm starting to think lying here and waiting for whatever fate awaits is probably a safer bet."

"And you'd leave Billy for me, would you?"

She felt those words like a punch to the gut. Launched herself forward, off the bed. Through the pain. Grabbed him with her one hand and pushed him back to that hollow wall. "You don't say his name. You don't even think about it."

Carlton smiled back at her. "Look at you. On your feet again. Looks like you've got more strength in those frail bones than you thought."

Aoife felt sick. Shaky. Weak. The whole launching herself at Carlton thing was completely reactionary. She felt dizzy. Needed to sit down.

But she wasn't showing any signs of weakness here. Not again.

"As long as he's out there. And as long as he's... as long as he's in danger. I'll fight for him. You might think you've got him. You might think you've won. But... but you're wrong. You're wrong."

Carlton's smile widened even more. "Now that's the fighting spirit I like to see."

He pushed her back. Gently. But strong enough to send her falling back onto the bed, which was a whole damned painful experience in itself.

"You sit back," Carlton said. "Your time will come. The two of us working together will make it easier for both of us. And besides. I want you alive anyway. It'll make that race to Billy even more exciting."

He turned around to that hollow wall.

Aoife had no idea what he intended to do with it. But he put a hand against it.

Then he pulled it back and buried his fist right into it.

Much to her surprise, the section of the wall he'd punched crumbled under his punch.

He looked back at her. Smiled as his knuckles bled. "See?" he said. "You should learn to trust me a little more."

He went to pull his fist back and punch the wall again when Aoife heard something else.

Footsteps outside the room.

The rattling of a key being turned.

And then the door opened.

CHAPTER THIRTY-SEVEN

The door opened, and a man stepped in.

Aoife hadn't seen this man before. Only person she'd seen here was Joyce. But this bloke looked far more intimidating than that old hag. Well, more *physically* intimidating, anyway.

He was tall. Very tall. Unnaturally so. So slim, with long arms right down to his knees. His chest protruded out at the front, and his face was narrow and bony.

And his face was grey, too. A deathly shade of grey.

He looked over at Aoife, and as their eyes met, she swore she *had* seen him before for a second.

A flash.

A flash of being pinned down by this man as he held onto her arm and...

Fuck. Yeah. He'd been there. He'd been there when they'd taken her arm off.

Maybe he'd even been the one to saw through her...

He looked right at Aoife. Time stood still. Carlton stood over by that hollow wall, not budging. Like he was hoping the bloke wouldn't see him.

But then he looked around. Looked at the dent in the hollow wall. Then looked at Carlton.

And before Carlton could do anything, he walked over towards him.

He reached out for him with those long, slender arms. He looked like the fucking Slenderman. He was creepy as shit. Didn't look the strongest guy. But the sheer height and length of him… he looked like he was going to wrap his limbs around Carlton like a damned octopus.

But there was something else that caught Aoife's attention.

The door.

The door to the room was open.

She could see the hallway outside.

And on that hallway, right by the door, a little tray with bowls and glasses on.

Bowls, glasses, and cutlery.

A knife.

She looked over at Carlton and Slenderman. Carlton was trying to dodge his grasp. Doing a pretty decent job so far, all things considered.

But then she looked back at that opening and wondered if she could use this opportunity.

If she had a chance.

She was weak. Exhausted. Fuck, she'd whinged about it so much at this point. But she definitely wasn't feeling any stronger. Worse than ever.

But she'd found the strength inside to stand up to Carlton just before.

If she could get to that door…

If she could just get to that door and get away…

A bang.

Slenderman had Carlton. Pinned him right up to that hollow wall.

Carlton looked over at her. Met her eyes for just a second.

And in that second, she looked back at him, and she knew that *he* knew what she was planning.

She knew that *he* knew exactly what she was going to try.

"Wait," he gasped. "She's—she—"

Slenderman covered Carlton's mouth with his hand and pushed him further back against that wall. Shit, he had more strength than she thought.

Which worked out perfectly for her right now.

If she could just find the strength to get off this bed and get out of this room.

She clenched her jaw. Took a deep breath. Even though she was dizzy, even though her head was spinning, she could do this. She could get out of here.

She had to.

She climbed off the bed and hobbled across the room.

Her movement was unsteady. Kept feeling out of balance like she was going to fall over.

But she kept on going.

She didn't even look at Slenderman or Carlton. But she was pretty sure he wasn't onto her.

She had a chance.

She could do this.

She could actually do this.

She staggered to the door. Went to take a left or a right? She didn't know. Couldn't be sure. Had no idea how she'd got in here.

But fuck. She had to pick a direction either way.

She had to—

A hand.

A cold, freezing hand on her back.

Pushing her right down to the floor.

She fell. Fell face-first onto the tray on the floor. Felt a glass smash beneath her.

And that pain.

That splitting pain from her arm, right through her body.

Those icy hands on her back.

He'd got her.

He'd fucking got her.

He turned her around like she was nothing at all. Looked down at her with those wide blue eyes. Held her down with those long, thin, bony arms.

Drool trickled from his chapped lips.

He smiled at her.

Smiled at her as she searched the floor for a piece of that broken glass.

As she tried to find a knife. Or a fork. Or just anything she could use.

But he had her well pinned down.

His smirk widened. That thick saliva fell onto her face. It stunk of vomit.

He didn't say a word. Just grunted as he pinned her down.

Holding onto her throat with those bony hands.

She looked over to her right. Over towards the nearest shard of glass.

And she tried to reach for it... then realised the very fucking arm she could reach for it with was gone.

Slenderman laughed. Like he knew what Aoife was trying to do. Like he understood how much shit she was in, too. Like he was enjoying it.

He tightened his grip. So tight now that Aoife couldn't breathe.

And if it weren't for Billy, she'd be happy to just give up.

Happy for the pain to end.

Happy to rest.

She tried to take a breath, tried to move, tried to resist the pain, when Slenderman's hands got even tighter around her throat.

And then she heard a thump.

A crack.

Slenderman's hands loosened.

Blood pooled out of his head, down his forehead.

His skull looked cracked like an egg.

He fell forward, face first, onto Aoife. Pinning her down with his surprising weight, considering his height.

And as she lay there, the taste of his blood on her lips, gasping for breath, she saw someone standing over him.

Carlton.

A blood-stained electric guitar in hand.

He smiled at Aoife. "I hope you weren't planning on going anywhere without me."

Carlton looked down at Aoife lying there on the floor before him, and he thought about killing her here and now.

But no. He could get a lot more satisfaction and a lot more enjoyment out of stretching this out.

The hunt. The hunt for Billy. That was where the real joy awaited.

And it was going to be *so* joyful. He couldn't wait.

He stood over the body of the dead freak. He hadn't got much of a buzz from whacking him over the head. Strange, really. He must be so desensitised to killing men that it just didn't really do it for him in the same way anymore.

And besides. He had his sights set on greater prey.

He thought about Billy. Thought about how he'd stalled before killing him. Thought about that resistance he'd felt inside. He'd had a chance to kill him. More than enough chances to kill him.

And yet... something stood in his way. Something stopped him.

"Are you going to just stand there?" Aoife asked.

Carlton smiled. Felt back in the moment, now. And he felt a little nervous, too. Nervous excitement, of course. Because they had a chance to escape. The pair of them had a chance to escape.

Is there really much use keeping her around?

No. He couldn't think like that. She was going to be useful. And besides. It was going to be interesting seeing how desperate she was to reach Billy. How desperate she was to find him...

Unless he's already in here.

It was a thought he'd had a few times. What if Billy was in here somewhere? What if he hadn't got away?

Where did they even begin searching for him?

That was another reason this woman was going to be useful. She knew Billy better than he did. So she'd have an idea where he was heading.

Yeah. It seemed like right now, keeping Aoife alive far outweighed the benefits of killing her here and now.

He could have far more fun with her before he killed her.

"Come on," Carlton said, holding out a hand. "The sooner we get out of here, the... Oh. I'm sorry. Wrong hand, again."

He held out his left hand instead.

She glared at him so hard he felt the daggers from her eyes piercing every inch of his body.

She stood on her own. She looked shaky and fragile like she might pass out at any moment. That would be unfortunate. Not the end of the world, but unfortunate.

He'd find his own way to Billy regardless. It'd just be more... well. Difficult.

"Sure you don't need a hand?" Carlton asked.

"Seriously," Aoife said. "Don't test me right now."

Carlton smiled. "You do realise that just makes me want to test you even more, right?"

She glared at him again. If looks could fucking kill.

"Look," she said. "Let's just... let's just get the hell out of here. Before it's..."

She toppled over a little. Put a hand on her thigh. Wincing. Holding her breath.

And Carlton wanted to watch her in pain.

He wanted to watch her struggle and suffer.

But at the same time... no.

He needed her for the hunt.

He went against all his instincts and walked over to her.

"You look like you could do with..."

It all happened so fast.

She swung at him.

Swung something sharp at him.

He grabbed her wrist—her one fucking wrist—and held it tight.

She held that piece of glass out towards his throat. So close. Just inches.

But she hadn't been able to strike him.

He squeezed her arm. Tight. Bitch. How dare she. He'd spared her, and this was how she repaid him?

And yet...

Well. She was bound to fight, wasn't she?

She was bound to stand up for herself.

Especially when Billy was at risk.

"How about you let go of this piece of glass right now," Carlton said. "And we forget this little slip up ever happened. Hmm?"

Aoife stared right into his eyes.

She kept on gripping onto that piece of glass. So hard that Carlton could see blood dripping down her hand.

"Unless you're dead set on losing another arm," he said.

She shook her head.

"Fucking prick."

And then she let go of the piece of glass.

Let it drop to the floor.

Carlton let go of her arm. It'd bruised already from how tight he'd been gripping it.

"Now," he said. "Let's start again."

He looked past Aoife, down the corridor. There were doors all around them. And then one right at the end of the corridor.

Outside, he could hear rain hammering down. Wind howling.

"Come on."

He walked towards that door at the end of the corridor.

"You sure it's this way?"

"Positive."

"And you're sure you're comfortable me being behind you?"

He looked around at her. Laughed. "I don't think you're dumb enough to try anything like that again. Now come on."

He reached the door at the end of the corridor. And what struck him was just how quiet everything seemed. It wasn't right. Something was wrong. No chance nobody had heard what'd just gone down.

There was something off.

He grabbed the handle. Held it for a little while. Put an ear to the door and listened.

"Nothing," he said. "Not a peep."

Aoife frowned. Or maybe that was just her default expression. A resting bitch face. And an active bitch face, too, for that matter.

Bless her. He wondered what she'd look like if he skinned that face away.

He'd soon find out.

"Come on," Carlton said. "I don't like this. But while we have the chance... it's our best shot."

She nodded.

He held his breath.

Turned the handle.

Waited a few more seconds so he was absolutely sure there were no sounds.

"Now," he said.

He pushed the door open.

He saw a kitchen/dining area. Kind of like an extension, with big glass windows lining the front of it, overlooking the fields, which were currently enshrouded in darkness.

There were bottles of alcohol everywhere, most of them half-finished, some of them smashed.

The smell of whisky hung in the air.

Whisky and piss.

He looked around this open plan living space, and the main thing?

There was nobody here.

So they had to make this count.

They had to make it count now.

He went to run through towards the door when he heard a shuffling sound, over to his right.

He stopped, and he froze.

The woman stood there. Joyce, she was called. The creepy old bint who he'd met just before they threw him in with Aoife.

She stood there with a shotgun in her hands.

"My boys," she said, snarling. "My dear, dear boys. You killed them. You murdered them. And you'll pay. Both of you will pay."

CHAPTER THIRTY-NINE

Aoife couldn't quite believe what she was seeing.

To be honest, she was starting to wonder if she was just fucking high on medication or blood loss or who knows what.

But as she stood in the doorway and watched Joyce pull that trigger on Carlton, she figured getting out of this place wasn't going to be quite as easy as first planned.

Carlton ducked and jumped out of the way with alarming speed. Shit. Maybe she *was* tripping. No way anybody could jump that fast in reality.

But hell. This was the reality she'd been handed. And she was going to have to work with it whether she liked it or not.

The shell dropped to the hard kitchen floor. Joyce shuffled along towards Carlton. She was crying. Snivelling away.

"You evil, evil swines," she said. "I only wanted to feed my family. I only wanted to feed my children. My dear boys. And look what you've done!"

She fired another shot over towards Carlton. And Aoife backed up. She saw Carlton in that kitchen, hiding behind the island. Saw Joyce marching over towards him, far faster than a frail old bint like her had any right to move.

"I was going to go easy on you," she squealed. "I was going to make it easy for you because I know how hard it is. But for what you've done... you'll suffer. You'll suffer."

Aoife took a step back. Went to close the door slowly. There had to be another way out of this place. There had to be another escape route.

And she could shake Carlton off while she was at it, too.

She went to close the door while Joyce's attention was distracted.

Then she heard a creaking noise.

The door. Creaking.

Comically louder than expected.

Fuck. Please don't notice. Please don't notice.

Joyce turned around.

Looked right at her.

Okay. Fuck. She's noticed. Right.

"Where the hell do you think you're going?" she shouted.

Aoife didn't even think.

She pushed the door shut and limped down the corridor.

A blast.

The sound of wood splitting.

The wood of the door she'd just closed.

Shit.

Shit, shit, shit.

Why did she think closing that frigging door was a good idea?

Not like it was going to frigging protect her or anything.

She rushed down the corridor as fast as her exhausted, weak body would allow. Heard Joyce shouting at the other side of the door. Heard her walking this way.

Fuck.

She had to hide.

She had to hide, or she had to escape.

One thing was for sure.

She had to get the hell out of here.

She tried the first door on the left, but it was locked. Then the next. Locked.

She saw the door she'd come out of. The one that one of Joyce's sons lay in front of.

Fuck. She couldn't go back in there.

Unless she used that guitar on Joyce. Waited around the side of the door then cracked it against her skull, just as Carlton did to her son.

Another blast.

The sound of the wall beside her cracking.

She was so close.

Shit.

She kept rushing down that hallway, feeling like this was probably the worst fucking decision in the world.

She turned the handle to the next door on the right.

And she prayed.

She opened that door.

It was unlocked.

She threw herself inside.

It was dark inside. She couldn't see a thing. Pitch black. No windows at all. Which meant there was no way out. Shit. Shit. Shit.

She felt around for something she could use. Something—anything—she could use to defend herself with. Or block the door with.

Footsteps marching down the hallway.

"I'll get you, you dirty cow. I'll get you, and I'll feed you your arm."

Shit. So they had used her arm as food. Aoife felt like throwing up. Hot bile in her throat. She was faint, and if she wasn't careful, she would pass out.

You've got this, Aoife. You've got this.

She searched around the room with her one frigging arm in the darkness when eventually she found something.

A shelf.

A shelf of some kind.

She could push that in front of the door. Block Joyce from coming in here.

And then what?

Fuck.

She'd get to that if she made it that far.

She went to push against the shelf. Strained to force it towards the door. The whole time, her entire body screamed out at her to stop. Especially her right arm. Or what was left of it, anyway. Shit. What was she doing? This had to be a bad dream. This had to be a nightmare.

She pushed that shelf more and more until eventually, she had to stop.

She backed away. Panted.

Stood still.

She couldn't hear any footsteps anymore.

Couldn't hear any voices.

But then she heard something else.

A knocking.

A knocking on the wall.

She turned around, and she saw a slight bit of light on that wall at the other side of her.

Shit.

The weak wall. The one Carlton punched.

Was he at the other side of it now?

Helping her?

Fuck. Did he have a literal death wish or something?

She heard a blast.

Heard a massive explosion.

Looked around and saw the door opening.

Shit.

She had to be fast.

She ran over to the wall and started tearing away at it with her one good hand.

Tearing chunks of it away.

Behind her, those footsteps got closer.

She pulled and pulled at the chunks from that plasterboard wall when suddenly she realised she hadn't heard anything for quite some time.

She stopped. The only sound was the blood racing through her head.

She didn't want to turn around.

She didn't want to see.

But she knew she had to.

She looked around and saw Joyce standing there.

Candle in one hand, illuminating her tear-soaked face.

An evil snarl.

"Too bad," she said. "I had real plans for you."

And then she pulled the trigger.

CHAPTER FORTY

Aoife squeezed her eyes shut.

She sat back against that plasterboard wall in the darkness.

She held her breath.

Because Joyce was standing over her.

Joyce was standing over her with a shotgun in hand.

It was over.

She was going to gun her down, and she was going to kill her, and it was all over.

She'd watched her pull the trigger.

And now she just waited for the shot that would end her pain, end her agony.

But she didn't feel anything.

Come to think of it, she didn't hear anything either.

Almost like she hadn't pulled that trigger at all.

She opened her eyes.

Joyce still stood there. Shotgun in hand.

She squeezed at the trigger, again and again.

But nothing was happening.

"Jammed," she muttered. "Stupid thing's..."

Aoife didn't hesitate.

She had no strength left. No fight left whatsoever.

But she wasn't giving this old bitch a chance to regroup.

She stood up.

Threw herself at her.

She knocked her off her feet. Sent her flying back to the floor.

Heard her head thud against the solid ground.

She punched her. Punched her repeatedly with her shaking left hand. Punched her in the face again, and again, and again.

Punched her until that shotgun dropped from her frail old grip.

And it was only then that she stopped punching her.

That she grabbed that shotgun with her hand, and she flung it over Joyce's head, again, again, again, until it cracked open and spilled blood everywhere.

It was only then that she stopped.

She sat over her. The smell of blood in the air. She realised her arm was bleeding, too. Badly. Worse than ever. Must've split a stitch. So the wound was open now. Which meant she didn't have long left at all.

"Wow," a voice said. "That was really... something."

Aoife looked around.

Saw Carlton standing over her.

He clapped his hands a couple of times, in jest.

"You look at me like I'm so different to you," he said. "But when I see what you just did here... I don't know. Maybe we're not so different at all."

Aoife went to stand. "We are different. Believe me, we are. Now how about..."

But as she stood, she went dizzy and fell back to the floor.

"Shit," Carlton said. "Don't want you dying on me just yet."

He walked over to her. Hovered over her. Her vision had faded. Gone blurry. Everything looked... bright. Even though it was dark. Everything had a strange light hue to it. A glow.

"Your arm. It's in a rather bad way."

"I figured that much," Aoife said.

"It's going to need stitching up. I've been known to be a dab hand with stitches in my life."

"What does that even mean?"

"It means, if you want to survive, you're going to need my help. Come on. Get to your feet."

She wanted to resist, but she didn't have the strength to. So she just let Carlton help her to her feet. Let him ease her out of the room, into the hallway, and then into the kitchen.

"On the table here," he said.

She didn't have the energy to resist.

"Now, they stitched you up before. So I'm sure they'll have something around here I can help you with. You just... wait there. Not that you're going anywhere anyway."

She listened to him step out of the room. Heard him rustling around in one of the side rooms. Close. But not too close.

Far enough away that she could try something.

See, she did feel weak.

And she did feel weary.

And she wasn't sure how long she had left, especially now her wound was bleeding again.

But she wasn't as weak as she'd been making out in these last few minutes.

"You hold in there, petal," Carlton called. "I'll be with you in a flash."

She tensed her fist.

Dragged herself up off that cold kitchen worktop.

Dropped down as quietly as she could.

Staggered across the floor. Towards those windows. Towards that door.

"It must be in here somewhere. And when I find it, we can get you stitched up... and then we can begin our hunt. Isn't that something exciting? Something to look forward to?"

She stumbled along.

Dizzy.

Faint.

But still awake.

Still aware.

Still alive.

"Ah," Carlton called. "Got it. I'll be right with you."

She grabbed the door handle.

Begged and prayed it wasn't locked.

And by miracle, the door slid open.

She pulled it along with what little strength she had left.

She felt the cold, icy breeze and rain crash into her.

She heard Carlton's footsteps coming back down the corridor.

"Coming, my love. Coming..."

And then she stepped outside and slammed the door shut.

She stood there in the dark. Stood there in the rain. Looked at the fields around her. The hills.

And as she stood there, freezing cold, in absolute agony, a tear rolled down her cheek, and she smiled.

Because she was free.

Even if just for a moment, she was free.

She thought about Billy.

Wherever he was, she was going to find him.

She took a deep breath.

Tensed her fist.

And as painful as it was... Aoife walked.

CHAPTER FORTY-ONE

The second Carlton stepped out into the open kitchen area, he knew he'd been double-crossed right away.

Aoife wasn't on the table. She wasn't anywhere he could see. He checked the sofa at the far side of the room. Checked behind the kitchen units. He checked literally everywhere.

But there was no sign of her.

She was gone.

He followed the bloody patches on the white floor. They led right over to those big patio windows. He felt his anger growing. At first, he'd almost admired her for having the courage to be so ballsy against him.

But this...

He was trying to help her.

He was trying to give her a chance in the hunt.

And she was just throwing it back in his face.

He walked over to those patio windows. Looked out into the darkness. Out into the night.

He took a deep breath, and he tensed his fists.

She could run. Oh, she could try running.

But she wasn't going to get very far.

Not in the state she was in.

He took another few deep breaths. *Calm down, Carlton. Everything's under control. Everything's going to be okay. She's going nowhere. And even if she does... there's absolutely no way she gets to Billy before you do.*

Unless she did.

Unless he let her.

A smile crept up his face. Irritation turned to excitement.

Maybe Aoife escaping wasn't such a bad thing after all.

Maybe he could lead her right to where he wanted to go.

Right to Billy.

He opened those patio doors.

Took another breath of that cold, rainy air and looked out into the storm, into the darkness.

"I'm coming for you, Aoife," he said. "And I'm coming for you too, Billy. Wherever you are."

He smiled.

Stepped out of this hellhole of a farmhouse.

And then he walked.

CHAPTER FORTY-TWO

Aoife had no idea how long she'd been walking when she finally collapsed.

She lay in the slushy, muddy ground. The ice had defrosted, and it was cold and damp and watery now. She was shivering, but she didn't feel cold. Didn't feel cold at all. She felt hot, if anything. Like she was in a sauna, and she couldn't escape the heat no matter how hard she tried.

She looked at her arm. Or rather, where her right forearm once was. She saw it was bleeding. And it was burning, too. Burning hot. Infected, probably. Just another thing to add to her already shitty situation.

She lay there. Laughed a little. It was typical, really. Things were always going to go this way. She'd known it for a while now, long before she lost a frigging forearm.

Even before she'd been struck by bloody lightning, she'd felt like shit. Her head just wouldn't stop aching. Probably a bleed on the brain or some crap like that. Hell, she'd never know. And it didn't matter either way.

The end result was the same.

She was screwed.

She lay there. Felt her heart beating irregularly. Maybe it was pumping its final few beats. She didn't know. Couldn't be sure. Again, didn't matter, really, did it? The end result would be the same.

For the first time, probably in her entire life, she'd actually begun to entertain the possibility that this might actually be the end of the road for her.

That she was dying here.

She was dying. And for the first time, she actually accepted that fact. Didn't *think* she accepted that possibility like in the past. But she actually realised that this was what was happening to her, and there was nothing she could do about it. There was no changing it.

The only thing she had now?

Figuring out what the hell she *could* do before the end finally arrived.

She looked up. Saw tall grass ahead of her. It was light now. So she must've been walking some way, at least.

She swore she'd heard things. Movement. Footsteps. Shouting. But she heard a lot of things when she was close to fainting, close to passing out, close to losing consciousness.

A part of her thought it might make things easier for her if someone just came over and put her out of her misery. Because at least it would be out of her hands then. At least whatever happened next would be out of her control.

But then... Billy.

She couldn't stop thinking of Billy.

She'd got attached.

She'd got herself frigging attached to that kid.

She knew that was dangerous. That was the exact reason she'd tried her best not to. Tried her best not to connect with anyone.

But then... what the hell was the point in anything if you didn't have someone to share your experiences with?

What was the point in life if you were the only survivor left?

She tensed her fists... or rather her fist. Still felt like she had the right one. Phantom limb. It really was a real thing.

She shook. Didn't have any strength left in her body. The thought of walking another step was exhausting.

But she didn't have a choice.

She pushed herself onto her knees and climbed back to her feet.

It was painful. Suffocating. Every inch of her body hurt. You get the frigging picture at this point.

But she kept on pushing through it.

Kept on forcing herself to stand.

She didn't know how she was going to do it. She didn't know how she was going to make it.

But she was going to fucking try.

For Billy.

She owed him that much.

She went to take a shaky step when she heard something right behind her.

First, footsteps.

Then, in her stomach, that familiar sense of dread.

And then she heard something she didn't expect.

A voice.

A familiar voice.

A voice that sent shivers down her spine.

"Aoife."

She froze. Heart beating faster.

No.

She couldn't be back.

She wanted to be alone now.

She was all in her head.

She couldn't think of her now. She'd only hold her back. She'd only beat her down. She'd only—

"It's you," she said. "It... it really is you."

But listening to that familiar voice—that impossible voice—Aoife started to wonder.

She started to wonder if it might actually be real.

If it might not be in her head.

No. It has to be in your head. The alternative is impossible. It's all in your head and—

She heard panting. Whining.

A dog.

She turned around as much as she was terrified and saw her standing there.

Saw all three of them standing there.

She looked skinnier. Her hair looked thinner. She looked exhausted, with big bags under her eyes.

But standing there staring back at her, she was unmistakable.

Rex by her side.

Billy by her side.

"Kayleigh," Aoife said. "Kayleigh."

CHAPTER FORTY-THREE

"Kayleigh," Aoife said. "I... It can't be you. It... it can't be you."

Kayleigh stood there. Tears streaming down her face. Her eyes were wide. Bloodshot. Big bags underneath. She had scars across her face. Scars and scabs and sores. The old attractiveness she used to have had been battered by God knows what.

But she was here.

She was standing here.

And as much as Aoife thought it might just be in her head, as much as she thought it might be in her imagination, as much as she told herself that this was impossible and couldn't really be happening... another voice—a louder voice—told her this was real. Told her this was true.

"I don't... I can't..."

"Aoife," Kayleigh said.

She walked over to her. Rex by her side. Even he seemed to be holding back. He wasn't darting over to her with the enthusiasm she expected. He wasn't racing towards her with happiness or joy.

He was holding back. Tongue dangling out. Ears raised, then

lowering. Stepping back, then forward, then back again. Whimpering. Whining.

"Rex," Aoife said.

He came, then. Came running over to her. Jumped up at her and knocked her down. He was too strong for her as he licked at her face. She couldn't handle his strength anymore.

But she didn't care.

She didn't care because he was here.

He was alive.

"I've missed you, lad," she said. "I've missed you."

She managed to finally drag Rex away from her and looked up at Kayleigh and Billy, who stood over her. Billy smiled at her. He looked so proud. He was okay; that was the main thing. He was okay and fuck, not only was he okay, but he'd found Kayleigh. He'd found Rex.

"This isn't real," she said to Billy, shaking her head. "This—this can't be real."

Billy looked at Kayleigh and shrugged. "Can't believe it myself. But it is real."

"'Fraid so," Kayleigh said. "Don't look too happy to see me. Anyway. What the hell's happened to you since I last saw you? You're missing a goddamned arm, in case you haven't noticed."

And Aoife laughed. She actually laughed. Even though she was in pain, even though she felt like she might drop dead at any moment now, she laughed.

"I'm sorry," she said.

"Sorry for what? For not giving me the best welcome?"

But Aoife wasn't talking about that. She wasn't talking about that at all.

She was talking about what happened eighteen months ago. Back at Sanctuary. With the power source.

Pulling that trigger.

Running away.

Standing right by the exit and watching as Kayleigh got swallowed up in flames...

"I watched you... I watched you die."

Kayleigh shook her head. "You did what you had to do. And as far as I can tell, I'm pretty alive. Not always so happy about that in this shitty world. But it has more pros than cons. And hey. Rex here has turned me into a dog person; I hate to admit."

Aoife shook her head and cried. "Yuri. I—"

"Yuri *was* blown to pieces, I can confirm. So you don't have to worry about him rising from the rubble, too. But yeah. I... I found my way. Wasn't ideal, but I did what I could. Did what I had to. And here we are. Another chance meeting. Kind of like fate wants to bring us together, isn't it?"

Aoife sat there and kept looking between them. Kept looking at Kayleigh, then at Billy, then at Rex, then back again.

Looking for any sign this might be a figment of her imagination.

Looking for any cracks that showed this might be in her head.

But she didn't see any.

She didn't see any at all.

"But I hate to rain on the happy reunion parade here," Kayleigh said. "But... you look like shit, love."

Aoife nodded. "Not a very nice thing to say."

"Maybe not. But you know I'm always honest with you. And it's true. We need to get you seen to. Somewhere. Somehow."

Aoife nodded. "I was... I was trying to get Billy to—to Rhyl."

"And you'd be better off not heading that way," Kayleigh said.

"What?"

"Went there myself. Tried to find you, actually. But... yeah. Let's just say it looks like Rhyl went the way of Sanctuary. Maybe worse."

Aoife's stomach sank. So that was one place in mind out of the question. Shit. To think she'd sent Billy that way, too. Even tried to send Polly's people there. That could've ended disastrously.

"So, where to?" Aoife asked.

Kayleigh smiled. Shook her head. "Isn't that the question?"

She walked over to her. Held out a hand.

"Either way, we need to get you on your feet. And we need to get away from here. That much we can agree on, right?"

Aoife grabbed Kayleigh's hand. Let her help her to her feet. "Right."

And when she pulled her up, she hugged her.

Felt the warmth of her body.

Cried some more, but with happiness. With total fucking joy.

She could've stayed in that hug forever.

But then Kayleigh moved her away a little, keeping hold of her hand.

"Come on," she said. "Let's get you somewhere safe. Safer than here, anyway. There's some strange folks about. And I really don't want to have to kill anyone else today."

She looked at Kayleigh. Then at Billy. Then at Rex. And as she stood there, exhausted and broken, she smiled.

"Let's go," she said.

She turned around with her friends, holding on to Kayleigh's hand, and she walked.

CHAPTER FORTY-FOUR

Carlton watched Aoife, Billy, and these two new additions—the woman and the dog—enjoy their beautiful little reunion, and he smiled.

He'd followed Aoife for a while. Wasn't hard. She left quite a trail. And she was slow as shit. She was in a bad way, so he could hardly hold that against her.

But seeing her now, seeing her happy—seeing her absolutely elated—meant that it was all worth the slow build.

Because it was going to make the next step all the more enjoyable for Carlton.

Aoife.

The woman.

The dog.

And the cherry on top, Billy.

He took a deep breath, and he smiled.

It was finally time to reap his rewards.

It was finally time to luxuriate in the joys of the hunt.

It was finally time to make them his prey.

CHAPTER FORTY-FIVE

Billy wasn't sure how long they'd been walking when he swore he heard movement behind them.

They were in some empty old city. There were rusty cars in the streets everywhere. The road was cracked, and he kept slipping and tripping up on it. He could hear birds above, crows cawing and swooping around. Some of them landed on the lamp-posts—the ones that were still standing—and looked down at them. Like even they were watching.

And there was something else that made him feel uneasy, too. Every now and then, he saw bones. He saw dead bodies. They had big wounds on their necks that looked like bite marks.

Or claw marks.

Like they'd been attacked by monsters...

He heard panting, then. Cursing. Looked around and saw Kayleigh. She was walking alongside him, carrying Aoife. Aoife looked like she was asleep. Like she'd passed out. She didn't look well at all. Looked like she'd lost a lot of weight in a really short space of time, and she was never really very big to start with.

He wanted to ask her if she was okay. He wanted to speak to

her. He hadn't known her for long, but he missed her. She made him feel safe.

But every time he got caught looking at her for too long, Kayleigh looked around at him. "Come on. Eyes ahead."

He turned around. Saw the dog, Rex, sniffing the kerb, then weeing against an old bin. He seemed a happy dog. He didn't seem to care about what was happening. He didn't seem to care about any of this.

And looking at Rex, looking at the crows, listening to them cawing... Billy wished he could be like them. He wished he didn't have to worry about anything.

Maybe when he got to wherever they were going, he wouldn't have to worry anymore.

And then he remembered what Kayleigh said. Rhyl. The safe place there. It had already fallen. It was no good.

And it made him wonder if maybe Aoife was right when she said there was nowhere good out there. When she said they were best on their own. On the road. Together, just the two of them.

Or maybe she hadn't said that. Maybe he'd just imagined she'd said that.

Maybe he'd imagined a lot of things...

But he was here. Right now, he was here with Aoife and Kayleigh, and Rex. And Aoife was sure they were dead. And even if they weren't, she was sure she'd never, ever see them again.

And here they were.

Proof that there could be miracles.

He took a deep breath of the cool air, and he looked back again.

He kept expecting to see someone. Kept expecting to see someone following. Because he'd heard someone.

And as he looked down this main road, he swore he saw movement. Movement between the buildings behind them. Movement around the cars. Movement all over.

And voices.

Voices and footsteps and...

"Hey."

He looked around. Snapped out of the moment again.

Kayleigh.

"Eyes ahead, kid. This place gives me the creeps. And with those goons lurking about back there... I dunno. The sooner we get someplace safe, the better."

Billy nodded, kept on walking. There was no point looking back. Even if there was someone coming, what did it matter? They'd need to get away from them anyway.

"Where is it we're even going?" Billy asked.

"Old medical centre just down here. Think it used to be an abortion clinic. But they've got other meds, too. Not many. But should be enough. And besides. Not many people know about it."

"But you do?"

"It's like I say," Kayleigh said. "People see an abortion clinic, and they don't expect there to be other meds stashed there, too. I found it out of chance. There's every chance someone else got there since I was there. But when I was last there, I managed to get some antibiotics down me. Some painkillers. Whatever Aoife needs, we'll get it to her. But I..."

She stopped. Her throat cracked a little. And Billy swore for a second that he saw tears in her eyes.

"What?"

She took a deep breath and then looked at Billy again like she was returning to Earth. "I just... I just want you to be prepared, Billy."

"Prepared for what?"

"You know exactly what."

She looked right at him with those tearful eyes, and he knew exactly what she was talking about right away.

Aoife's death.

She was weak, and she was struggling. And this wasn't going to be easy.

And even if they got to this medical centre and got Aoife all the medicine she needed, there was still no guarantee she would be okay.

She'd been through a lot. A hell of a lot.

She was missing half an arm now.

This wasn't going to be easy.

Billy didn't say anything else. He just nodded.

Nodded and turned to the road ahead.

"We get her there," he said. Feeling stronger. Feeling more confident. "We get her medicine. We bandage her arm again. And we fight for her. 'Cause—'cause that's what she would've done for us. It's what she'd always do for us."

Kayleigh looked down at him, and she smiled. "You're a tough kid, you know?"

Billy opened his mouth. Went to disagree.

Then he felt the opposite.

He felt that same strength he'd felt climbing up that slope towards safety on the train tracks.

He felt stronger.

He *was* strong.

He'd survived this far.

And he was going to keep on surviving.

Not just surviving, but helping those he cared about survive, too.

"I know," he said. "But I... I wouldn't be this strong without the people around me. None of us would be."

Kayleigh's smile widened. "Amen to that."

She looked ahead, holding shakily onto Aoife. "Now come on. We've got to get to that medical centre. Before it's..."

She stopped.

Looked ahead.

Stared into the distance at something.

Billy's heart started beating fast. His stomach sank. "What is it?"

"Be still."

"What—"

"Be very quiet and be very still."

And Billy didn't know what Kayleigh was talking about.

Not at first.

And then he saw it, and every inch of his body turned to stone.

The orange and black fur.

Those massive paws.

A tiger.

There was a tiger in the street ahead of them.

CHAPTER FORTY-SIX

Billy saw the tiger in the distance, and it felt like he was seeing the monster he'd been so, so scared of all his life—only for real now.

It was beautiful. Its fur was so bright and orange. And the black was dark, dark as the night sky. It must've escaped a zoo. It looked bigger than it looked on television or in a zoo. There was something about seeing it here, wandering through a street, that made it seem even larger.

And it was scarier, too.

Knowing there were no bars between him and it.

Knowing nothing was stopping it attacking him and Aoife, Kayleigh and Rex.

"Keep very still," Kayleigh said. "And when it looks away, we're going to back off. We're going to back off very, very slowly. And we're going to hide."

Billy could barely breathe. He could barely think. He wanted to run, but he felt stuck to the ground. He felt like his feet were frozen. Or like he was pinned down.

He couldn't run as much as he wanted to run.

But staying still... staying still was the most dangerous thing ever right now.

He watched that tiger. Closely.

Watched it wander around between the cars, sniffing the air.

And it felt like a nightmare. It felt like a bad dream.

He heard something behind him.

Shuffling.

Footsteps.

Spun around.

Nobody there.

Nothing at all.

"Billy," Kayleigh whispered, holding tightly to Aoife. Rex stood there, very still. Not even growling. Just totally still. "Be quiet. Very quiet. And..."

She stopped speaking.

Or maybe she didn't stop speaking; Billy wasn't sure.

Because the tiger looked right over at him.

It stared at him. Stared with these big amber eyes. It must've got out of a zoo. It was big, but it looked... come to think of it, a bit bonier than the tigers at the zoo. A bit skinnier.

He thought of the bodies he'd seen. The smell of death in the air.

He thought of the bones lining the street.

He thought of it all, and he wondered if they'd walked right into this tiger's trap.

"It's seen us," Billy said. "It's..."

He didn't get to say anything else because the tiger started running towards them.

He didn't even think.

He didn't stay still.

He *couldn't* stay still.

He turned around, and he ran.

He heard a roar somewhere behind. He heard shouting and running. And he just had to keep running. Running past the cars.

He had to get into one of the buildings. He had to get away. He had to hide.

He looked over his shoulder, and he saw Kayleigh running too. Aoife in her arms. Rex in front of her. Didn't look like he was standing up for himself right now. Looked like he had the same idea.

And that tiger, chasing behind.

He saw them all running from the tiger, and as much as he wanted to get away, he wanted to help them, too. He didn't want to leave them behind.

He was strong.

He could do something.

He couldn't just run.

He looked to his right as his heart raced and his body shook, and he saw a car right beside him.

He grabbed the handle to the back door.

Opened it up.

Then looked up.

"Get Aoife in here," he shouted.

Kayleigh frowned. "What?"

"Just—just get her in here. Then we—we keep going."

He pulled that back door open.

Stood there, as they all got closer.

And then he turned around when he knew it was too late to do anything else about it.

Kept running.

Kept on going and going and hoping everything worked out, hoping everything went to plan.

He heard a shout, a cry, and he felt his stomach sink.

He looked back.

The door to the car was shut.

Aoife was nowhere to be seen.

Rex was running along towards him.

But Kayleigh was on her back.

She'd fallen over.

She had her knife in hand. She was swiping it at the tiger.

But the tiger didn't seem to be stopping.

It was still coming towards her.

He needed to do something.

He couldn't just run away.

He needed to get to her.

He needed to think.

He looked around and saw one of the dead bodies at the side of the road.

Flies buzzed around it. It smelled bad. Looked a few weeks old.

But could he use it?

Could it help here?

He had to try.

"Here goes nothing."

He grabbed the loose flesh from the man's arm. It fell away with horribly surprising ease.

He held it in its hand, all coated in maggots, and he looked around at the tiger as he hovered over Kayleigh.

"Hey!" he shouted.

The tiger looked up. Turned its attention from Kayleigh.

Looked right over at Billy as he stood there, holding the dead meat.

"Billy," Kayleigh said. "What the hell are you doing?"

"Leave her alone!" Billy shouted. Feeling terrified. But also feeling stronger now. Feeling like he was doing the right thing. Because so many people had done so many things for him. And now it was his turn to help them.

The tiger tilted its head. Growled a little.

"No," Kayleigh said. "What—"

"Leave her alone!" Billy shouted.

He stood there. Watched, totally still. Watched as the tiger stared back at him. As Kayleigh lay there, bleeding from her head.

He watched her try and lift the knife and saw the tiger swat it away. Accidentally? He wasn't sure.

But she didn't have a weapon anymore. She was defenceless.

He saw Rex by his side. Growling now. Standing beside him. Beginning to bark.

And he stood there with that rotting meat in his hand. Shaking.

But feeling stronger than ever.

Just as strong as he had to be.

"Come on," he said. "Come get it."

Tears rolled down his face as he awaited the end.

But at least it gave the others a shot.

He saw that tiger look down at Kayleigh once more.

Then back up at him.

And then, out of nowhere, it began to run towards him.

CHAPTER FORTY-SEVEN

Billy watched the tiger launch itself at him, and he knew it was time.

He didn't feel afraid anymore, as he stood there and watched it get closer. Of course, it *looked* scary. And, of course, he knew it wasn't going to do nice things to him. He knew this wasn't going to go well. He knew it was going to be painful, and he knew he was going to die, and he knew it was all going to be over much sooner than he thought it was.

He wanted to grow old. He wanted to leave school and get a job and go around the world and get married and have kids and then be a granddad someday.

But he knew, as he stood there, tears burning his eyes, that he wasn't going to get any of that anyway.

Because this world was different.

This world was never going to get better.

Things were never going to be the same again. Things were never going to be back to normal ever again. And the sooner he could get used to that, the better.

But at least he had this.

At least he could help people who had helped him.

At least he could be strong for them.

He'd been through horrible things before. He'd been scared so many times before.

At least this time, he could do something to help.

He watched the tiger get closer. Heard it roar so loud it made his body vibrate. He saw its teeth, so big, covered in saliva. And even though it was scary, he couldn't hate it. Because it was just hungry. And it was just doing what it had to in order to survive. It wasn't evil. It wasn't like people. It wasn't doing it for fun, power, or control.

It was doing it because it had to do it to survive.

And he couldn't hate it for that.

"Billy!" Kayleigh shouted.

He heard Rex barking. Heard Kayleigh crying out.

But he just stood there, and he stared that tiger in its eyes.

"It's okay," he said. Shaking. Shivering. He could smell wee, and he knew he'd wet himself. "I know—I know you just have to do it. I know—I know why. It's okay."

He saw the tiger staring right back at him.

He saw it roar again and smelled its ghastly breath.

"Billy," Kayleigh said.

He looked past the tiger at her. Saw her by the car he'd told her to hide Aoife in.

At least they had a chance to get away.

"You've got to go now," he said. "You've got to... to get to that medical centre."

Kayleigh shook her head. Went to say something.

He didn't see what.

Because the tiger jumped towards him.

He closed his eyes.

He held his breath.

He thought of...

Well, of Aoife.

He thought of Aoife holding her arms around him. Telling him everything was going to be okay.

"It is," he said. "For you... for you, it is."

He waited for that tiger's teeth to wrap around his throat when suddenly he heard a bang.

A growl. A whimper. It didn't sound angry anymore.

It sounded... wounded.

He opened his eyes.

The tiger was backing off. It was bleeding from its right paw. Limping away, off behind the cars.

He stood there and watched as it backed off. As it disappeared. And he couldn't get his head around it. He couldn't understand. Where was it going? What was happening? What was that bang? What'd happened?

He watched the tiger roar and then disappear again as he stood there with that rotting meat still in his hand.

Kayleigh stood in front of him. Crouching by the car. Rex by her side.

They were both looking over at him with wide eyes.

"What..." he started.

Then he realised they weren't looking *at* him at all.

They were looking at where that bang came from. The one that scared the tiger off. A gunshot? It seemed that way.

He turned around slowly and saw him.

He was holding a gun.

Walking towards Billy.

Smiling.

And as much as he hated it, he felt more afraid by him than he did by the tiger.

"Hello, again," Carlton said. "Now. Where were we?"

The real monster was here.

CHAPTER FORTY-EIGHT

Aoife opened her eyes.

She felt like total shit. Which wasn't a major fucking surprise. She'd felt like shit for God knows how long.

Speaking of which... where the hell was she? She was lying down. How'd she ended up lying down all of a sudden? The last thing she remembered, she was... Wait. What *was* the last thing she remembered?

She remembered...

Fuck.

Losing her arm.

Escaping Joyce's place with that psycho, Carlton.

And then...

"Kayleigh," she said. "Rex. Billy."

She squinted around, then, taking in her surroundings for the first time. She'd found Kayleigh and Billy and Rex. But then... something must've happened. She didn't have many memories. Only of walking. Of feeling so, so fucking weak, and... no, not walking. Being carried. Hovering somewhere. Floating.

And then she remembered shouting. Crying.

And then...

Nothing else.

She looked around properly. She was in a car. Lying across the back seat. The door opposite her was closed.

She lifted her aching neck a little. There was nobody else in here with her. The car was empty. The windows were all intact, which was something.

But where the hell was she?

For a moment, she wondered. What if the last few years were all a dream? What if she was waking up after that bus crash in some debris of a car that'd flown into the bus or something?

But no. It didn't make sense. Didn't make sense at all.

And besides. Looking at her arm right now—or rather, her lack of arm—it was pretty clear things were as she remembered.

She reached for the door handle. Shuffled herself around. Opened the door then climbed out into the sunlight.

She was in the middle of a town somewhere. Abandoned. Loads of cars. Signs of foliage taking over again, plants climbing their way up the sides of buildings, that sort of thing.

And as she stood there, in the cool breeze, she suddenly became aware of just how alone she was.

What'd happened here?

Where was Kayleigh? Billy? Rex?

Where were the lot of them?

She stood there and looked at the road for something—for any sign of where they might be or where they might've gone to—when she saw something that made her stomach sink.

Blood.

Blood, on the road, right at her feet.

And a trail.

A trail leading over towards the side of the road. Through a maze of cars.

She gulped. Swallowed a lump in her dry throat. She was going to have to go look. She was going to have to investigate. Even if she found something she really, really didn't want to find, she would have to look anyway because she needed to know where the hell they were. She couldn't be alone again. About time she stood up and admitted that. Especially not the physical state she was in.

"Kayleigh?" she called. "Billy? Rex?"

She walked. Followed that blood trail. Her vision was all blurry. Her balance was all over the place. She felt wearier than ever. Like she might just collapse onto this road and never wake up again. Why the fuck was it taking so long? If this was death, then why wasn't she dead yet?

"Anyone?" she called. "Is... is anyone..."

She heard something, then.

The other side of the car.

The car where a large pool of blood stared up at her in front of.

A growl.

She stood there. Barely able to breathe.

There was something behind that car.

Growling.

Rex?

No. Too deep for Rex. Something else.

Something bigger.

She stepped around the car slowly.

When she saw what was there, she could barely believe her eyes.

A tiger lay there. A fucking massive tiger, staring back at her. Growling.

Only it was wounded. Bleeding from its paw. Badly.

She felt bad for it. As surreal and as fucking terrifying as this whole situation was... she felt awful for it. She wanted to help it. She wanted to do something for it. Even though she knew there was absolutely nothing that could be done.

She saw it looking up at her, wounded, and she thought it saw itself in her, too.

Wounded.

On its last legs.

Just seeking one final source of comfort.

"I'm sorry," she said. "I just hope..."

She saw something, then.

Something that sent shivers down her spine.

Right beside the tiger, she saw something familiar.

That black shirt with the little skull on it. The one she'd grabbed for Billy in the shop the other day.

Lying right beside the tiger's mouth.

Covered in blood.

Torn.

She gasped. Stumbled forward towards the tiger a little bit.

Because...

No.

It can't have killed him.

That can't be what happened here.

Unless...

She remembered the shouting. The screaming. Those memories, in a haze.

Had it attacked them?

Had it killed them?

She remembered Kayleigh throwing her into the back of that car.

A flash of a memory.

"Don't you go anywhere," Kayleigh said.

Then the tiger roaring and—

"No," Aoife said.

She stood there opposite the dying, bleeding-out tiger, and she just stared at it. Stared at it as it growled. Stared at it as it tried to move. Stared at it as more and more blood oozed out onto the ground below.

And as she stared at it, she started to understand what'd happened.

Exactly what'd happened.

Kayleigh.

Billy.

And even Rex.

They were gone.

The tiger had attacked them, and they were gone.

She tensed her fist, and suddenly her pity for the tiger disappeared.

Suddenly, it was replaced with rage.

She looked around for something she could use.

Something she could kill it with.

Something she could punish it with.

Because it'd killed her friends.

It'd killed the people she loved.

She yanked a chunk of solid metal debris from the car beside her.

She stood over the tiger. Sharp, rusty end of the metal in hand.

"Nobody touches my people," she said. "Nobody... nobody touches my people."

She lifted the metal and went to ram it towards the tiger's head when it let out a little whine.

It sounded like a cat. Like a poor defenceless cat.

Looked up at her.

And for a moment, for a split second, she saw fear in its eyes.

She felt bad. And then she dropped the metal to the ground.

Cried.

Stood beside that tiger and cried.

Because it hadn't done it on purpose.

It'd done it in an attempt to survive.

Wasn't that all any of them were doing, after all?

She stood there in her loneliness, and soon knew her time

would be up. She wished she'd had a better ending. She wished things could've gone better for her. That life could've been easier. And that she had people beside her right now, in her loneliest moment.

But then she remembered something, as she stood there, swaying on her feet.

She wasn't lonely at all.

She'd *had* people beside her.

And they were still here.

Still right here with her, in her heart.

She stood opposite that tiger as her consciousness grew less and less concrete, and she took a deep breath.

"Whatever's next," she said, "I'm ready for it. Whatever's next, I..."

She heard something, then.

Out of nowhere.

Cutting through the silence of this abandoned, empty, decaying town.

Clapping.

She turned around slowly. Looked around to where the clapping was coming from.

Walked around the car so she could see.

And when she did see, she froze.

Carlton was standing there, smile on his face.

Clapping.

And at his knees, two people.

Kayleigh.

Billy.

Both of them bound around their wrists.

Both of them gagged.

Both of them staring up at Aoife with fear in their eyes.

Carlton stopped clapping, and he chuckled.

"Hello again, Aoife," he said. "Pleased to see me?"

CHAPTER FORTY-NINE

Aoife saw Carlton standing there with a gun to Kayleigh's head, Billy kneeling by her side, and she wished she had a bit more strength right now.

The sun shone down brightly from above. Must be late morning or early afternoon. She didn't know. Didn't particularly care in all truth. She felt freezing cold, but she was sweating at the same time.

The streets around were quiet. Empty. The usual post-apocalyptic sights: rusty old cars, tall grass, glass all over the place. Boarded up windows. Graffiti smeared across the walls: HELP US.

Silence. Silence but for the crows cawing above, their cries echoing through the emptiness.

She could smell rot in the air. The sour stench of death. So strong she could taste it. Might've made her heave once upon a time when she was less used to it.

But it was just so commonplace now. It was just a part of everyday life.

She stood there, shivering, and looked over at her two friends.

Kayleigh and Billy were both bound at the wrists and the legs, by the looks of things.

They were gagged. Kayleigh looked like she had a few new bruises under her eyes. Billy, on the other hand... oh Billy. His face was pale. His eyes were distant. He looked like he'd retreated to that place he'd been when Aoife first found him. That detached look to him. The place he went to when things got too much for him.

And could she blame him?

This psychopath had a gun to him and Kayleigh.

And Rex was nowhere to be seen.

"You thought you could just walk away, didn't you?" Carlton said. "Thought you could just wander right on away. After the things I did for you. After I helped you."

"Cut the bullshit, Carlton," Aoife said.

Carlton laughed. "See, that's what I like about you, actually. You aren't afraid to trust your gut. You're ruthless. Totally ruthless. But how you played *this* game... it wasn't very sporting. I set the rules, and you broke them. And you thought you could win by breaking the rules? You think anyone has ever won by breaking the rules?"

"I think you should put that fucking gun down right now," Aoife said. "It's not about these two. It's not about any of us. But... but if you're gonna start making threats towards the people I care about, then you'll have to go through me first."

She walked over to him. Limped, rather. Keeping her back tall. Tensing her one fist. That agony in her phantom arm still crippling her.

Carlton looked back at her. Narrowed his eyes. Smile widening. "Wow. Aren't you a confident one?"

"Kayleigh and Billy don't deserve whatever you've got planned for them. They've—they've been through enough. I'm standing right here. Right fucking here, on a plate. So whatever psychopathic urges you have... just get it done with. But get it done with, with me. Or at least try, anyway."

Carlton lowered his gun. Shook his head. "You know... I really do admire that. Honestly. That level of selflessness is rare."

He lifted his gun, and this time, he pointed it at Billy's head.

"But it's foolish," he said.

He tightened his grip on the trigger.

"Wait!" Aoife cried.

He didn't keep on pulling that trigger.

He loosened his grip on it.

Laughed.

Looking more animated than she'd ever seen him.

She looked at this monster, and there was only one person she could think of. Only one person in her life she'd known who'd come close to this degree of depravity—pointless depravity.

Her brother. Seth.

And she hadn't known how to play him.

She'd never known how to get the better of him.

He was always one step ahead of her.

Unless...

"I... I don't know what you've been through to make you this way. I won't—I won't pretend to understand, either."

Carlton's eyes narrowed. A more serious look took over his face.

"But... but I don't believe people are born like this. Whatever happened to you in your past... I'm sorry. I really am. I won't—I won't judge you for it. And I won't judge you for this, either. But you need to put the gun down, Carlton. You need to put it down. Because... because if you don't, then it'll be on your conscience forever."

Carlton laughed. Snorted. "On my conscience? You really think that's something I lose sleep about at night?"

"Yes," Aoife said. Head spinning. Still dizzy. Still struggling every damned second to stay on her feet. "I... I think you do. I don't think you like to admit you do. But I think you do. I think you spend every waking moment of your life wondering why you are the way you are. I think you torture yourself for it. I think it taunts you. This—this sick addiction of yours. But there's still time. That's the beauty of this world. Don't you see? In all the darkness... that's the real beauty. There's still time. Because nothing stains this world. You can reinvent yourself every single second. You can—you can walk away from here. And we can walk away from here. And we can be different people. We can start again. Even after everything, we can start again."

Carlton stared at Aoife. Tears welled up in his eyes.

"You know what, Aoife?" he said. "That might just be the nicest thing anyone has ever said to me. I thank you for that."

And then he lifted his gun and pointed it at Billy's head.

"And that's why it's even more important he dies."

It all happened so fast.

He went to pull the trigger.

A growl and a bark, from over to the right.

Carlton turning around, his eyes widening with fear as Rex launched towards him.

Carlton turning that gun on Rex, and—

"No!" Aoife cried.

She ran at Carlton as Rex jumped up at him.

She ran at him as Carlton turned his gun, staggering back.

And then she heard a bang.

CHAPTER FIFTY

Aoife heard the bang, and she knew it was over.

Rex.

Rex flying through the air towards Carlton.

Carlton turning that gun on him.

Watching his finger tighten around the trigger, in slow motion.

Only...

No.

She landed on Carlton.

Tackled him to the ground.

And that's when she heard the bang.

She lay there. Lay on top of Carlton. She didn't feel cold anymore. She felt warm. Like it was a warm summer's day. The sun beaming down so strong from above. She swore she could hear waves crashing against a shore somewhere close by. She could smell sun cream and hear children laughing. Feel the sand between her fingers...

And then she tasted the blood in her mouth and felt the burning pain in her stomach.

She blinked. Blinked those gritty eyes and saw Carlton staring back up at her.

Smile on his face.

And then she looked down.

She looked down towards where she was hurting, and she realised.

She understood.

Blood.

Blood pooling out from her stomach.

Pooling out far heavier than it'd ever pooled out of her—and ever pooled out of anyone she'd seen.

She felt dizzy. Felt fucking sick. Wanted to vomit everywhere. In an instant, she went cold again. Very damned cold.

She looked back up at Carlton as he held that gun to her stomach, and she watched his smile widen even more.

"You see?" he said. "You can't fix everybody. You can *think* you can. But you can't. Some people don't want to be fixed, Aoife. Don't you see that?"

He pushed her back, then. Pushed her away.

She fell onto her aching back and clutched her stomach with her one hand.

And as she lay there, completely broken on the cold and muddy ground, she wanted to get up. She wanted to fight. She wanted to get to her feet and stop him.

Because he was walking over to Billy and Kayleigh and Rex.

He was walking over to those people she cared about.

Those people she loved.

He was walking over to them, and they were in danger.

Her ears rang. Her head spun even more than it did before. She tried to stand, but she couldn't. She was totally wrecked at this point.

"See, I appreciate what you said," Carlton said, walking over to Kayleigh and Billy, pacing from side to side. "Really, I do. I don't believe you had any motives. I believe you meant what you said.

You're a very honest and gracious person. And you're a fighter. A fighter for what you believe in. I respect that."

He lifted the pistol and pointed it at Kayleigh's head, then.

"But what you didn't realise is that I can't be fixed because I don't want to be fixed. Because why would I? Why would I choose any other life than the one I have? I don't get to choose anyway. This... this feeling. I can't escape it. But you know what? It's worth it. It's so, so worth it."

She watched him hover that gun behind Kayleigh's head, and she waited for another bang. Waited for a crack of a skull. Waited to watch someone else she cared about die right before her eyes— and just after she'd been reunited with her, too.

But no.

Fuck that.

She wasn't just going to watch.

No matter how much pain she was in, no matter how much she was bleeding, she wasn't going to just watch.

She pushed herself up. Her left arm gave way, and she fell back down. The muscles in her stomach spasmed and resisted, making the bleeding even worse as she tried to get to her feet.

She felt pain, and she felt weakness, and she felt totally defeated.

But she pushed on.

She pushed on despite every inch of her body screaming at her to give up.

"I won't... I won't give up," she said.

Carlton watched her. Even he wasn't smirking anymore. He looked genuinely surprised. Genuinely amazed.

She tried to straighten out her shaking, sore, exhausted knees. Blood pouring out between her fingers. That taste of metal still so strong in the back of her throat.

"I won't... I won't give up," Aoife said. "I won't ever give up. Not on... not on the people I... the people I love."

She took a painful deep breath, and she stood.

She looked at Carlton. Looked at Kayleigh. She looked at Billy, and she looked at Rex.

And as she stood there, there was so much she wanted to do.

She wanted to stay standing.

She wanted to fight.

But she knew that's exactly what she *was* doing.

She knew they could see that.

She knew Kayleigh and Billy and Rex could see that.

And she knew everyone that had fallen—everyone she'd blamed herself for losing—could see it too.

"That's sweet," Carlton said, sighing. "Really, really sweet."

He looked down at Billy. Smirked.

And then he looked back at Aoife and lifted his gun.

"But to be honest, I'm getting kind of bored of your dramatics."

And then he pulled the trigger again.

Aoife heard the bang.

She felt the splitting pain in her chest.

And as much as she tried to stay on her feet, as much as she tried to stay standing, she fell back and hit the ground.

CHAPTER FIFTY-ONE

Billy watched Aoife hit the ground, and he wanted to scream.

He'd shot her. Carlton had shot her. Not once, but twice. First time, she'd got back to her feet, bleeding badly. She looked so tired. She looked so weak. She looked so, so sick.

But she'd stood back up.

And seeing her standing there, even though he knew it was bad, even though he knew nothing good could come from everything that was happening... Billy looked into her eyes, and he felt so proud of her for how strong she was.

For standing up.

But it wasn't her who needed to stand up anymore.

It was him.

He and Kayleigh.

And that's why he kept on scraping the ties against the ground while Carlton wasn't looking.

Getting them looser and looser and looser.

And just waiting for that perfect moment.

But now, things felt different. Aoife lay on the road before them. Blood pooled out from her stomach and her chest, spreading across the ground. Billy's ears rang. He couldn't hear anything anymore from the gunshot. He could see Carlton's lips moving, but he couldn't hear it, not now.

He could smell smoke. Death.

And then eventually, he started to hear something. Rex, barking. That deep bark of his.

He wanted him to shut up. He wanted him to be quiet.

Because he didn't want him to get shot too.

He saw Carlton standing over Aoife. Staring down at her. And it was weird. It was weird because he looked like he was totally fixated on her. Looked like he was totally transfixed by her.

Like he was soaking up this moment.

And it creeped Billy out even more.

He looked over at Aoife. Heart beating fast. She was so still. Not moving at all anymore.

And he knew he needed to be quick.

He knew he had to get these ties from around his wrists.

And when he did... he knew what else he had to do.

He could see it right between them. That piece of glass. Long. Sharp.

Just what he needed to ram into Carlton's throat.

Just what he needed to end all this.

He looked down. The ties were loosening. But they weren't loose enough. Not yet.

They were still around his wrists. Still too tight to break out of.

And when he *did* break out of them, there was still his ankles...

This wasn't going to be easy.

But he had to try.

He had to.

He looked up and saw Carlton looking around at him now.

His eyes were wide. And he had this sinister smile on his face. He looked like drunk people looked when they'd had too much to drink. Like he was in a daze. Like the killing had changed him. Made him... jollier.

"Now," he said. "Where were we?"

He walked over towards Billy.

Gun in hand.

Walked over to that piece of glass.

His foot hovered over it, just for a second, and Billy thought it would come down on it and smash it and ruin his plan completely.

But something else happened.

His boot kicked it just a little.

Not so it was mega close to Billy.

But it was closer.

It was within reach.

If he could just get these ties off...

"You know," Carlton said. "I would lie to you and say I really didn't want to do that. Or something like that. But like I say. That would be a lie."

He took a step closer.

Right in front of Billy.

That piece of glass just between them.

He stopped.

Looked down at Billy.

Smiled.

"You don't look afraid," he said. "Why don't you look afraid?"

And Billy could tell something. He could tell from the sound of Carlton's voice that he didn't like that Billy didn't look afraid. He could tell that Carlton got off on people being afraid. Like some of Ramiro's people.

But the more Billy saw of Carlton... and as much as he was scared for Aoife... he wasn't afraid at him.

He stepped up and put the gun to Rex's head.

"How about now, huh? Feeling spooked now, kid?"

But Billy just stared up at him. He just kept his eyes on him. Just watched.

"No?" he said. "No. You really are something else, ain't you?"

He lowered his rifle, and then he stood there a few seconds. Looked down at Billy. Eyelids twitching.

And Billy made sure to look at Carlton at all times.

He didn't want to look at the glass.

He didn't want to give it away.

And then Billy heard something.

A sound.

A splutter.

Aoife.

She was lifting her head again. Trying to stand. Trying to get to her feet.

Carlton rolled his eyes and turned around. "Oh, why won't you just die already?"

And at that moment, as Carlton walked over to Aoife and booted her in the stomach, making her scream, as horrified as Billy was and as scared as he was and worried for Aoife as he was... he reached forward.

Grabbed that glass.

And then he moved back.

He cut at his ties.

He broke his hands free.

He looked around at Kayleigh. Heard her mumbled cries. Saw the tears down her face.

And then he looked back up at Carlton.

Walking back over towards him.

"Never learn, you lot. Never. But you'll learn now. And people'll keep on learning. Because that's just how it goes. That's just the way the world works."

He stopped. Right in front of Billy. Crouched down, right before him.

"I was wrong about you," he said. "I thought you were different. For a moment... I dunno. Some weird part of me thought maybe I *could* be a better man. But you know what?"

He paused a few seconds.

"I don't want to be a better man. 'Cause what's the fun in that?"

He smiled at Billy. Put a cold, bony hand to the back of his head.

"You look like you've got something to say, kid," Carlton said. "Why don't you go ahead and say it?"

He pulled Billy's gag away.

Looked right into his eyes.

"Go on," he said. "What is it?"

Billy took a deep breath and gritted his teeth. "You need to watch out for broken glass a lot more."

Carlton's eyes narrowed. "What..."

Billy lifted the glass and buried it into Carlton's chest.

He stabbed him. Stabbed him hard in the heart.

And then he stabbed him again, and again until he was on his back.

He stabbed his hands as he tried to lift them to protect his face.

He stabbed his neck.

He stabbed his face.

And he didn't stop stabbing until he was absolutely covered in blood.

Carlton lay there. Bubbles of blood spurting up from his lips.

He was smiling.

"You... you *are* different," he gasped. "You're... you're like me. You're..."

"I'm nothing like you," he said.

He spat on Carlton, and then he buried that piece of glass into his neck once more.

He held it there. Held it there as Carlton's weak, shaking arms swatted at him. As he tried to push him away. Tried to fight back. As he coughed up more and more blood.

He lay there with tears rolling down his face as Carlton's fighting grew weaker and weaker.

He held it there until Carlton went totally still.

And then he stepped back.

He wasn't afraid anymore.

He was strong now.

CHAPTER FIFTY-TWO

Billy stood over Carlton's dead body, and he didn't feel anything.

The sun was bright. The air was warm. Or maybe that was just him. Maybe he just felt warm because of what had just happened. Because of what he'd just done.

Maybe it was the crusty blood all over his body, getting dryer and dryer.

He could feel it in his eyes. Taste it on his lips. Smell it in the air. And he could see it, too. Carlton. Carlton lying there before him, barely recognisable anymore. Completely bathed in red. Like he'd been dipped into a big tub of blood and dragged out of it.

His face was covered with lots of open wounds. So too was his chest. Billy could see those stab wounds everywhere. He knew he'd stabbed him a lot. He'd stabbed him, and he hadn't stopped going.

But he didn't know he'd stabbed him this much.

He looked down at him as he stood there, and he didn't feel hate. He didn't feel guilt. He didn't feel fear.

He just felt... like this was right.

He took a deep breath and turned around.

Kayleigh was still tied up. Rex was by her side. Tilting his head. Wagging his tail a little. But he looked more nervous of Billy now. Less sure of him.

He didn't want to look back again. He didn't want to see Aoife lying there. He didn't want to remember what'd happened. Not now.

So he walked.

Walked over to Kayleigh. Cut her free of her ties.

Even she flinched away, just for a second. Like even she hadn't seen that coming. Like even she didn't think Billy had it in him.

He pulled her gag away. And he looked down at her.

She stared up at him. Quiet. Opened her mouth a few times and closed it like she was struggling to find the words to say.

And in the end, she just closed her mouth and nodded.

He nodded back at her.

That's when he heard the cough.

He froze. A shiver crept up his spine.

He couldn't be alive. He'd stabbed him so many times. No way could he still be alive.

But when he looked around, he realised it wasn't Carlton at all.

"Aoife," he said.

He ran over to her side. Kayleigh and Rex along with him.

She was lying face flat in the road. A large pool of blood underneath her.

"We need—we need to get her help," Billy said, trying to turn her around. Suddenly coming back to his senses. Like a cloud was lifting. The same deadening cloud that descended over him when those men were doing those horrible things to him.

He was *feeling* again.

He was afraid again.

Kayleigh just stood there. Staring at Billy and Aoife with wide eyes.

"Kayleigh," Billy shouted. "We—we need to do something. We need to help her!"

But Kayleigh wasn't moving. And deep down, as much as it hurt to admit it, Billy knew exactly why.

"Please," he said. "Please."

Kayleigh walked over. She helped Aoife onto her back. And it was only when Billy saw her face that it really sunk in just how sick she was.

She was deathly pale. Her skin was as white as the moon against a night sky. She was shivering really badly. The wound on her stomach was bad. And the one on her chest. She was bleeding really, really badly.

And her eyes... they looked like they were somewhere else. Like *she* was somewhere else already.

And then, for a moment, just for a moment, they connected with Billy's, and she smiled.

"Aoife," Billy said. "We're—we're here. We're not going anywhere."

He held on to Aoife's hand. The other arm, where it'd been cut away, was bleeding again too. And looking at her, seeing what she'd been through, seeing how she'd stood up and kept fighting all this time... he saw how strong she was. He saw how brave she was.

"You saved us," Billy said. "You... You saved me, and you saved us. I'd still be with those people if it wasn't for you. And I'll—and I'll save you too. I won't leave you. I promise."

He knew he couldn't promise that. He knew it was going to be hard to save Aoife. Seeing her right here, he knew it would be impossible.

But he wasn't going to leave her side.

He was going to hold her hand.

He didn't want to let her go.

He heard her take a deep breath. Raspy. Sounded like she didn't have many breaths left.

She pulled Billy closer with that shivering hand.

Leaned in towards his ear with all the strength she had.

"You... you are brave. And you are... you are strong. You saved... you saved me. You saved me."

She kissed him on the cheek with her dry lips. And then she lay back, back against the road. Lay there with a smile on her face. And as Billy crouched there, tears stinging his eyes, he saw how peaceful she looked. How content she looked. How happy she looked.

"We saved each other," Billy said.

Aoife's smile widened, then. A tear rolled out of the corner of her eye, tinted with blood. "We... we saved each other," she said.

He kept hold of her hand and kept crouched beside her. Kept on telling her everything was going to be okay. Kept on telling her he was here. Stayed right there, by her side, as Kayleigh stroked her hair, as she whispered to her, too.

He watched as Rex walked over. As he perched himself beside her. Lay down on his paws. Stared up with those big sad eyes and let out a little high-pitched cry before sighing.

He kept hold of Aoife's hand until it finally went loose.

Until her grip loosened completely.

He kept hold of her hand as she took her last breath.

And he kept hold of her hand when she went completely still, and he knew it was over.

He knew Aoife was gone.

CHAPTER FIFTY-THREE

Aoife lay on her back and stared up at the sky, and she felt more comfortable than she'd ever felt in a long, long time.

It was bright. And it was warm. She couldn't feel any pain anymore, even though she knew she should be in pain. Even though she knew every inch of her was hurting just a moment ago.

None of that seemed to matter anymore. All of that seemed to blend into the background. Blend into total irrelevance.

She was comfortable now.

One thing she did feel was that warm hand in hers. It could be anyone's hand. Max's hand. Kayleigh's hand. Dad's hand. Seth's hand.

But whoever's hand it was... it felt comfortable.

It made her feel safer.

"It's okay," a voice said. Childlike. Almost angelic. "You're going to be okay. We're right here..."

And then Aoife realised who it was. Billy. Billy was right here, right by her side. She could hear him crying, but she didn't want him to be upset. Now wasn't the time to be upset.

Now was the time to be happy.

Because he was here.

He was alive.

He'd made it.

And he had a chance.

She squeezed back against his hand. It took a lot of effort to do so. But she did it anyway.

She knew she didn't have much effort left in her. She knew there was no point conserving any of it. Not anymore.

She knew she might as well do whatever made her feel comfortable. Whatever felt right.

Because she knew she didn't have long left.

She felt a hint of sadness. Just for a moment. A twinge of fear.

Because this was it.

All the odds she'd fought against, all the times she'd been cornered, all the times when she'd felt like it was her final moment, and this was actually it.

And she pictured the life she could've lived. She pictured herself working in conservation over in Africa, with elephants and lions. She pictured herself meeting someone out there and living a life of happiness with them.

She pictured the life she could have lived in all its gorgeous, high-definition glory.

And the most amazing thing?

The thing that cut right through every bit of fear and every bit of nostalgia, and every bit of regret?

She wouldn't change the life she'd had for anything.

She thought about her time with Max and Rex. She thought about her time in Sanctuary. She thought about Kayleigh and Billy. She thought about all of it.

And even though there was sadness, even though there was loss, Aoife felt nothing but a deep gratitude for the life she'd lived.

Because she could see it now.

She could see it clearly.

She hadn't let anyone down. She hadn't let anyone die. She hadn't failed anyone. Anyone at all.

She'd always stood up.

She'd always fought for other people. She'd always fought for what she'd believed in.

She saw Rex in need of a saviour from his horrible former life.

She saw Max at a low ebb, lost in life, not wanting to connect.

She saw Kayleigh when she came across her again, all her faith in outsiders shattered.

And she saw Billy.

She opened her eyes, just a little. Looked into those tearful eyes of his.

And as she stared up at him, she found herself smiling. Smiling through the lump in her throat.

She pulled herself close to him. Pulled herself up to him with all the strength she had, the little, minuscule strength she had.

"You... you are brave. And you are... you are strong. You saved... you saved me. You saved me."

And then she kissed him and fell back against the road.

Billy looked down at her. Tears streaming down his face now.

But he was smiling, too.

"We saved each other," he said.

And Aoife felt a weight lift from her shoulders when he said that. She felt a sense of relief. Like a cloud was rising from above her, and for the first time in years, she could see properly again. See with a real sense of perspective.

"We... we saved each other," she echoed.

She closed her eyes. And she felt something, then. A warmth, right beside her. A little whine. Rex. Curled up to her like he was hugging her. Like he was comforting her.

She wanted to say so many things to him. She wanted to thank him so fucking much for being there. She wanted to apologise for not being able to spend longer with him since their reunion.

But that was how life went, sometimes. That was just the way things went.

And she was lucky she'd even had a chance to spend any time with him at all.

She was lucky she'd had any time with anybody at all.

Because not everyone was as lucky as she was.

She felt his fur against her skin. Felt his chest rising and falling, his breathing against her body. And she breathed in unison with him. She breathed in sync with him. Still holding on to Billy's hand. Holding on for as long as she possibly could.

And then she felt a warmth against her ear.

Someone else. She recognised her smell.

Kayleigh.

"I don't... I don't know how to say this," she said. "And I... I don't even know if you're still listening. And I... I wished it could've happened some other way. But I never thought I'd get the chance. But now... now I do. Now I do, and I wish things could be different, but I... I love you, Aoife. I love you. I always have. And I—I always will. I wish I'd told you earlier. I wish I'd... I wish I'd told you at a better fucking time. But I love you. More than you'll ever know. I'm sorry."

Aoife felt Kayleigh's tears drip onto her face, and that drop of sadness sank in her stomach. She knew Kayleigh had a thing for her. She suspected she was probably in love with her. She'd known for a long, long time. But she'd tried to push it away. She'd tried to resist accepting it. Because it wouldn't work. It could never work.

But lying here, right now, hearing those words... she felt nothing but love too.

"I love you too," Aoife said. "Always."

She felt Kayleigh's lips against hers.

She felt a warmth inside.

She felt an explosion of happiness, and relief, and of joy.

And she didn't feel sadness anymore.

She felt lucky.

She felt so, so lucky.

She looked up. Looked up and saw them all there, with total clarity now.

Saw Billy beside her.

Saw Kayleigh beside her.

Saw Rex beside her.

And behind them both, she saw someone else standing there.

Smile on his worn, bearded face.

Max.

"It's your time, kid," he said. "Never thought I'd say that. Never wanted to have to say it. But it catches up with us all eventually, huh?"

She nodded. Swallowed a lump in her throat. A bittersweet taste in her mouth. That final memory of Max. Of how he'd died. Of how Grace had killed him...

"There are so many things I wish I could say to you," Aoife said. "So many things I've wanted to say to you all these years. Things I never said."

His smile widened. "Well. Now you'll get a chance. You ready?"

Aoife's heart raced fast. She saw the people around her fading... or rather disappearing into the brightness. She felt a tingling sensation, not unpleasant, all over her body.

She saw a bright light beaming down from the sky above.

She looked up there, and she felt some resistance. An instinctive sense of resistance.

She wanted to pull back.

She wanted to fight.

She didn't want to leave these people she was here with.

She didn't want to leave her friends.

"But you're not leaving them, Aoife," Max's voice said. "You'll always be with them. Always."

She took a deep breath. And she knew as much as she wanted

to hold back, as much as she wanted to resist... there was no point in fighting. Not anymore.

It was time to rest now.

It was time for the next step.

She looked at Billy. At Kayleigh. At Rex. One final time.

And then she looked at the light ahead.

"I'm ready now," she said. "I'm ready."

And then the light surrounded her, bathed her, lifted her up, and took her away to somewhere peaceful.

She wasn't suffering anymore.

CHAPTER FIFTY-FOUR

Billy looked down at Aoife's dead body, and he knew it was over.

The sun was out. It felt warm, now. The warmest he'd felt in a long time. It was quiet. Silent. Not even the sound of birds. He could smell blood on his skin, rusty and metallic. And he could taste it, too. Blood and salty tears.

He looked down at Aoife as she lay there, and he still couldn't quite believe it.

She was on her back. Her eyes were closed. And there was a smile on her face. She looked happy. Peaceful.

Kayleigh sat by her side, feeling her neck. Checking for a pulse they both knew wasn't going to be there. It felt like she'd been there checking for a long time.

But she finally looked around at Billy, and she nodded.

He felt his stomach sink. He felt more tears start to flow. He hadn't known Aoife for long. But she'd helped him. She'd given him a chance. She'd made him believe in himself. Made him realise he was stronger than he thought.

And he wanted to thank her for that. It didn't matter that he'd only known her for a few days. It was enough.

Sometimes you only know people a short amount of time in life, but they can still make just as big an impact on you.

He saw Rex, lying there right beside her. He looked sad. Like he didn't want to move. And Billy got it. He wanted to lie down and curl up beside her, too. Because this didn't seem right. This didn't seem fair.

But they weren't going to be staying here.

They couldn't just stay here.

There was something they had to do.

He looked up. Over at Carlton's body. And he felt so much hate towards him. He remembered standing over him. Stabbing him, again and again, and again, and how good it'd made him feel. How angry it'd made him feel.

How powerful and strong it'd made him feel...

He wished he could do it again. He wished he could do it to everyone who'd ever hurt him before.

That anger boiled away inside him, getting hotter and hotter.

And then he realised he was bleeding from his hands because he'd been digging his fingernails so far in, and he stopped.

Kayleigh stood up. Stood right there beside Billy as they both looked down at Aoife's body in the middle of this abandoned town.

"We should take her somewhere," Kayleigh said. "Bury her. Even though it's not what she would've wanted."

Billy smiled as more tears trickled out. "She—she would've wanted us to keep moving. 'What good's looking after my body when it's dead?'"

Kayleigh laughed. "Yeah. That sounds like Aoife to me."

They both picked her up regardless of what she'd want. They carried her out of the middle of the town and took her to a little park area just outside. It was nice here. Quiet. Nice big trees, and it felt pretty sheltered, too. And it didn't seem like there was anyone about. Didn't seem like there'd been anyone about for some time.

And then they dug.

They dug through the sun. Dug through the rain. And they didn't stop digging for a long, long time. Felt like hours.

And when they were done, they both lifted her over that hole and dropped her down into it.

She lay there so peacefully, still. Such a happy look to her face.

And as much as he missed her, as much as he was going to miss her... Billy knew she'd died standing up for people she cared about.

And in his short time of knowing her, he knew there was no other way she'd want to go out.

"You just wait there a sec," Kayleigh said. "Something I want to go grab. Something I think she'll like."

She walked off. Billy waited by the grave in the wind, Rex by his side, whining. After a while, as he stood there, he started to get afraid. The wind grew a little louder. He swore he saw movement in the branches. Was someone here? Was someone watching?

And then Kayleigh returned.

She walked over to Billy's side, holding something he didn't recognise at first.

Not until...

"Is that..."

He didn't have to ask.

The paw.

The paw from the tiger.

"She loved animals," Kayleigh said. "And tigers were her favourites, I think. She was trying to get into zoology when all this shit happened. If she knew she'd end up buried with a tiger's paw... well. She'd want to know the ethical implications. But she'd still be pretty stoked."

Billy didn't know what she meant by "ethical implications." But he was glad Aoife would be buried with something she loved. That seemed pretty cool.

"Goodbye, pal," Kayleigh said, throwing the paw down into the grave. "I'll miss you. I—I really will miss you."

He looked down at her, down into the ground.

And then he reached into his pocket.

Pulled out that Freddo wrapper. The one from the train.

He threw it down. Watched it drop towards her body, dancing in the breeze.

"Goodbye, Aoife."

And then they buried her.

Billy didn't say anything to Kayleigh while they were digging the soil back onto her. He wanted to. Every now and then, she just started crying. And he wanted to ask if she was okay.

But she didn't look like she wanted any questions. Not right now.

He knew she just needed some time.

They finished burying her. Stepped back from the grave. Looked down at it as the sunlight peered into this park.

"There," Kayleigh said. "All that fuss for you, Aoife. You'd better bloody appreciate it."

They stood there together a while. Just stood there in the warmth of the sun. Staring down at that grave. Billy thought about the first time he'd seen Aoife. And when he'd heard her speaking to herself—imagining Kayleigh and Rex were still here.

He was so glad she'd found them again before she died.

He was so glad she'd had that peace.

"What now, kiddo?" Kayleigh asked.

Billy looked up at her. He felt nervous. Scared. And he didn't know whether he could make any choices. He didn't know what was next. He didn't know where they were going to go. He just knew things were going to be different from now on. Very different.

He looked down at Aoife's grave, and he tensed his bloodied fists.

"We survive," he said. "For Aoife."

Kayleigh smiled. "For Aoife."

They looked back down at that grave once more.

"For Aoife," Billy said again, with his shaking voice.

And then they turned around, Rex by their side, and they walked away into the sunlight.

Towards whatever future lay ahead.

Towards whatever awaited them.

They were going to survive this world.

They were going to make the best of it.

For Aoife.

CHAPTER FIFTY-FIVE

Somewhere in the distance, Oliver lowered his binoculars and he sighed.

He would find his son.

He would find his Billy.

One day, he would find him.

And he'd never stop believing that.

END OF BOOK 8

Rise From Darkness, the ninth book in the Survive the Darkness series, is now available.

If you want to be notified when Ryan Casey's next novel is released—and receive an exclusive post apocalyptic novel totally free—sign up for the author newsletter: ryancaseybooks.com/fanclub

www.ingramcontent.com/pod-product-compliance
Lightning Source LLC
Chambersburg PA
CBHW060529160726
47991CB00001B/244